JERK

An ABCs of Love Novel

by

Amazon Bestselling Author

Daryl Banner

JERK

An ABCs of Love Novel

Copyright © 2022 by Daryl Banner
Published by Frozenfyre Publishing

All rights reserved.

No part of this publication may be used or reproduced in any manner whatsoever, including but not limited to being stored in a retrieval system or transmitted in any form or by any means, electronic, mechanical, photocopying, recording or otherwise, without the written permission of the author.

This book is a work of fiction.

Names, characters, groups, businesses, and incidents either are the product of the author's imagination or are used fictitiously. Any resemblance to actual places or persons, living or dead, is entirely coincidental.

Cover Model – Carlus Tyler Reed

Cover Photographer – Eric Battershell Photography

Cover Design – Nicole Blanchard

Interior Design – Daryl Banner

For all of the nice guys out there

and maybe some of the jerks, too.

;-)

Chapters

Prologue.. 1

1. Nice Guys 3

2. Profile Pic 8

3. The Setback 17

4. Swipe Right.. 26

5. Popcorny.. 34

6. Open Minds 45

7. Wingman 54

8. Buzz 62

9. Games 71

10. The Dog 81

11. Bad Guys.. 95

12. You're Sweaty 108

13. Tough 114

14. Weak... 128

15. Hard-To-Get.. 136

16. Friends?... 145

17. Ride... 161

18. Jerk... 171

19. The Mirror 179

20. Perfectly.. 188

Epilogue 213

Prologue

YOU DON'T WANT A NICE GUY.

Just admit it.

The real guy you want to sweep you off your feet isn't wearing a fucking cardigan.

He doesn't laugh at all your jokes. He won't remember your anniversaries. He won't bring you hot chocolate on a cold night, or stay up with you to watch that last episode of whatever binge-worthy show you're into, or cuddle with you under some dumb fluffy blanket.

And still you're madly in love with him.

Why? Is the sex really that good?

Why don't you want the nice guy? The one you can actually take home to Mom and Dad? The one who smiles with his eyes, who *will* laugh at your jokes—even the bad ones? The one who will hold you after a hard day, who will run to your side even if it's inconvenient, who will cherish you like a precious glass thing and worship you?

Instead, you seem inexplicably thirsty for only one type of man:

Jerks.

1

It's inevitable that guys like me lose hope in ever finding love. Capturing your heart isn't easy when the world is full of countless jerks you're so willing to give it to. I've grown colder with every date, with every unreturned call, with every "it's not you, it's me".

What's a nice guy to do when he's playing a game you won't let him win?

Is this how bad boys are born? Are they all just former Mr. Nice Guys who gave up? Can love really be such a sadistic, double-edged blade that laughs with every drop of blood it draws from another brokenhearted fool?

To tell my story properly, we have to start at the end.

As in: the end of the Mr. Nice Guy I used to be.

1. Nice Guys

MY BACK SLAMS AGAINST THE KITCHEN WALL.

A plastic bowl and a spoon topple from the counter nearby and crash to the floor.

His big hands slip around my waist and pull me against him with need, then glide farther down to greedily cup my ass, which he has seemed rather obsessed with since we left the restaurant. He complimented it six and a half times—the "half" because he was interrupted by a police siren whizzing by.

This is my latest "Mr. Nice Guy", by the way, a date I recently swiped right on. It's interesting that ten minutes ago, he was just telling me he likes to respect a man and take things slow. He said he's looking for love, just like I am. Not a fling. Not a quickie. He said all the right things.

They always do.

I should've known what I was getting myself into.

Especially because it's clear what *he's* getting himself into: my pants, as they pop open, unzip, and drop to my knees. And then he drops to his, slips me into his mouth, and

I throw my head back with a happy, naïve little sigh.

According to our profiles, we both like Italian food, cats, and obscure off-Broadway musicals such as *Job of the Century*. That title carries an amusing double entendre at the moment.

Getting sucked off in your kitchen isn't usually how you meet your husband.

Just as I get acclimated to the amazing sensation of whatever his tongue is doing down there, he grabs hold of my hips and spins me around. My face presses against the wall with a surprised grunt—and his face presses between my cheeks, tongue darting out to show me yet another talent he forgot to mention on his profile. Unless this files under the "I'm a jack of all trades" remark in his About Me section.

This is probably the part of our love story we'll omit to our kids someday.

The date had gone perfectly, by the way. We did the dinner thing at a low-key fancy place (i.e. somewhere affordable yet nice enough and easy to worm out of if it goes south). I laughed at his jokes and smiled when he complimented my "intentionally messy yet stylish" hair. I asked all the questions and he gave all the answers. I paid the bill, we had a cute and awkward exchange, and I agreed to let him come back to my place for a nightcap.

I guess I didn't expect the nightcap to be my asshole?

"Do you want to take this to your room?" he asks after coming up for air.

How courteous of him to ask. That's another tidbit on his profile, by the way: he's '*courteous*'.

In another blink of an eye, we're on my bed and he's on top of me trying to work a condom down his shaft. He bites his lip impatiently as he frowns at his cock and the condom that stubbornly won't roll down the right way, like it's letting him down.

And it only takes this much of a break in our momentum for me to lift my head off the pillow and express my doubts. "I think we're going at this kind of fast."

He stops and turns his face to me, confused. "Fast?"

"I ... I don't usually do this on a first date. I sorta thought we'd just hang out a bit, finish up our chat from the restaurant and, like ... call it a night, maybe?"

The look on his face suggests I'm speaking Dothraki. "Huh?"

"I know, I know. I almost said something earlier, but ... everything happened so fast, and suddenly you were eating out my ass, and then—"

"I thought you were into this." He gestures at his washboard abs, as if to remind me I can wash my dirty clothes off on them when we're finished. "I thought this was where we were going all night long. With the dinner. With the wooing. With all the *nerdy-stuff* chat you made me sit through."

I blink. *Made him sit through ...?* "I thought you liked nerdy stuff."

"Yeah, of course I do ... when it leads to *sex*."

"I just don't think I can go all the way. I'm not really into hooking up on the first date."

"Seriously? For fuck's sake. Even wasted a perfectly

good condom." He sighs and flings it to the side, giving up on it. "Should've known."

"Known what?"

He's off the bed the next instant and yanking his clothes back on. "That you're one of *those* guys."

I'm so bad at arguments, half the time I don't even realize I'm in the middle of one. "What guys?"

"Some kind of psycho cock-tease trap." He thrusts his shirt on with such force, I hear threads pop. "Stringing me along all evening, fooling me into thinking this night had a happy ending, flirting and being cute. If I stayed, next thing I'd know, I would've woken up in the morning with a ball and chain hooked to my foot and a ring on my finger. *No thanks*." He crouches down to shove his shoes on.

"I ... I'm sorry. I swear I wasn't trying to lead you on. I even paid for dinner."

"Yeah, and I'll pay for *this* mistake with blue balls all night." He rolls his eyes and gets to his feet. "I'm getting the hell out of here."

"But I thought ..." I'm at the edge of the bed—and the end of my rope. It's been a long time since I invited anyone up. A very long time. I confess I had high hopes for tonight. Maybe I should curb the tinge of desperation in my voice. "I thought we had something. You said you were looking for a boyfriend."

"That's what you're supposed to say. That's what *everyone* says." He stops at the door and gives me a withering look. "Thanks for dinner."

I blink at him, at a loss for words.

Is it too late to change my mind?

The sound of his footsteps tramp down my hallway, and then I hear the rattle and the slam of the door to my apartment. Silence surrounds me like a cold, wet hug I didn't ask for. A moment later, it's permeated only by the muffled racket of the hot couple next door—on the opposite side of my bedroom wall—who start going to town on each other with total abandon. I listen to the framed picture hanging on my wall as it rattles from the unapologetic thumping.

Well, at least someone's getting some tonight.

2. Profile Pic

"MAYBE YOUR DATING PROFILE IS MISLEADING."

"My what?"

"Your profile. Hmm, let me look."

The office is quiet today, except for me and Prisha, my best friend and perpetually beautiful coworker. She has long black hair, smooth dusky skin with warm olive undertones, and eyes that can instantly pierce any lie and reveal your secrets. Or at least that's what being her friend feels like at times like now. I can't keep anything from her. I think that's why I trust her so much.

She squints as she thumbs through my phone, elbows propped up on the table. "Hmm, I think it's your profile pic," she decides. "It isn't wholesome enough."

I lift an eyebrow. "Wholesome …?" We're supposed to be researching marketing trends of a certain demographic—male gamers, ages 14 to 16, to be exact—but apparently I wouldn't stop complaining about my date last night. "I don't think 'wholesome' captures a lot of attention, and—"

"You're correct. It doesn't. But it captures the *right*

attention, and isn't that the point?" She eyes me with those all-knowing eyes of hers. "Isn't this literally the kind of work we do every day? Fine-tuning demographic targeting to make the firm's marketing campaigns more efficient?"

I frown. "You can never turn off the marketing eye, can you?"

"Cast too wide a net, and you'll attract all the wrong guys." She taps on a photo, then slides my phone back to me from across the table where we're working. "Use this one instead."

I stare at it. "Are you kidding? A cardigan? That's me last year at Halloween."

"It's cute. Besides, the love of your life won't know the difference. Or at the very least, he'll think you have a sense of humor. Or it'll be a nice talking piece for dinner." She lifts her own eyebrows at me. "Rome, when you ask for my advice, then bat it away like a dollar store cat toy, it makes me question why I give you advice at all."

"I know, I'm sorry, but I—"

"Attract the *right* guys. That's all you need to do. The rest is just icing on the cake." She winks at me, then returns her attention to her laptop. After a moment, she bites her lip. "Ugh, now I want cake."

I stare at the picture on my screen—me in a cardigan doing some kind of "secret serial killer" professor thing, though the serial killer part isn't really apparent, which I guess was the point—and I try to imagine being the kind of guy who swipes right on it.

Am I trying to attract secret serial killers?

Stuffy professors?

Does Prisha really know me at all?

Do I?

A shadow falls over my workstation. I glance up to find Mr. Milton—our immediate supervisor—standing over me. He is literally the word "douchebag" fashioned into physical male form. From his stiff dress clothes, to his shiny watch, to his perfect hair, to the mug of coffee he's always sipping, to the condescending way he talks, to the sheen of his cufflinks. Douche, douche, douche.

"Is this yours?" he asks.

Whenever he talks to me, he doesn't even look at me; he just stares at the sheet of paper in his hand, which likely holds a list of trending keywords and hash-tags I compiled for him an hour ago. "Yes, sir," I answer him, "it is."

"Hm." He purses his lips after taking the daintiest sip from his mug. "Hm." He squints at it.

I take a patient breath. "Is something wrong with the list, sir? Do you need more?"

He smacks his lips. "The letters are tiny. This is printed in 11 point. I need 12 point. Are you *trying* to kill my eyes?"

"Oh, sorry. I didn't realize I—"

"Save your excuses for someone who has time for them." He drops the paper onto my keyboard. "I need a new list on my desk in five minutes." He saunters back to his office, his shiny dress shoes squeaking noisily with each step.

As I get to work reprinting the list in a font size that's exactly *one* point bigger, Prisha gawks at me. "Mr. Milton has a lot of nerve. 11 point and 12 are basically the same."

"Not really. And it's fine," I insist. "The poor man has … sensitive eyes."

"You're way too nice. I hate the way he speaks to you."

"Hey, if I want that promotion to team leader—which comes with a raise—I'm going to need to do all I can do to impress him. If that means reprinting a dozen lists in bigger font sizes, I'm all for it."

Prisha smirks at me. "And remind me, how long exactly have you been waiting for this theoretical promotion?"

Two years. I just give her half a smile. "I gotta finish this in five minutes. Actually, two and a half now." Then I resume my work without answering her question. After a sigh and a shaking of her head, she does the same.

The marketing firm we work for—*Bold Brands Marketing Firm*—is situated cozily on the seventh floor of an office building on the busy cluster-fuck intersection of 29th and Quincy Street. When five o'clock rolls around, Prisha and I take the elevator to the first floor, where we engage in a post-work activity that's become our way to blow off steam:

Hitting up the gym.

It's called Jesse's Fitness. Don't ask who Jesse is. No one knows, and no one's met him, but he's got a privately-owned gym leased out on the first floor of the building our marketing firm is in. And after being offered discounted memberships, of course a number of us took the bite. So there I am, running on side-by-side treadmills with Prisha, plus three others from the office who joined us today, including our friend Juan.

Well, the term "running" is being used loosely here; we look more like five bored soccer moms powerwalking.

11

Actually, even "powerwalking" is stretching it. We've got our phones out, skimming our social media feeds, and cracking jokes to each other about the latest trending hashtags. Even when we're at the gym blowing off steam, we're still working. We're the opposite of the usual clientele, which seems to be buff gay men. We spend an hour at the gym every day and don't ever break a sweat.

"I'm going to shower at home," says Prisha after our hour's up and she gathers her things to go, wrapping her pink-corded ear buds around her hand. "Are we still on for Dakota's party this weekend?"

"Definitely. Can you cover a gift from us if I pay for half? You know I'm bad at—"

"Gift-giving, yes, already have it covered. The gift's free, courtesy of my mother and her obsession lately with making beaded jewelry, so you owe me nothing. The jewelry is right up Dakota's alley." She hoists her bag over a shoulder. "You really are such a terrible gift-giver. Do you remember where I got these?" she asks me, lifting her pink ear buds. "You. Birthday, last year. And I got you a bag of that imported candy from India you like, plus that reversible pink-blue octopus plushie you probably snuggle with every night. You're lucky you've got me."

"Sorry," I say with a wince. "I'm terrible at gifts."

"Don't get me wrong, of course. I obviously love them. They're the only ear buds I use." She pockets them and winks at me. "Are you coming?"

A muscled guy in a sweaty white tank top walks past us, heading for the locker room. He seems to have no awareness of how much space he takes up in an aisle, because Prisha and I both have to step out of the way so as not to get knocked over, and he barely notices. The aroma of his sweat mixed with his spicy deodorant intoxicates me. "I'm ... gonna shower here," I decide rather spontaneously. "I'm pretty sweaty, and I ... could use some extra time to think. Y'know. About profile pictures and stuff."

Prisha, of course, pierces straight through my lie—but clearly chooses not to acknowledge it. "I'll see you tomorrow then. Don't get into any trouble, Rome."

"In the shower ...?" I ask innocently, then grab my backpack and head off.

The men's locker room in an obscure gym like this is likely just what you expect: poorly lit, full of some serious male funk, and a lot of men either sizing each other up or checking each other out—or both. And as I shove my stuff into a locker and get ready for a shower, my eyes devour a dozen different flavors of muscular gorgeousness. Sweaty chests. Puffy arms. Tight, toned abs. Broad shoulders. Wide backs. Calves like baseballs and asses like basketballs smuggled within drenched gym shorts. I'm barely paying attention to what I'm doing, my eyes too busy everywhere else. My heart is racing before I even make it to the showers.

A half-naked muscled guy reeking of sweat carelessly bumps into me as he walks past. Either he doesn't notice or doesn't care, but his elbow knocked me enough to illicit a wince. Even still, my instinct is to apologize for being in the way. He meets up with a buddy of his across the aisle, the pair of them laugh about something, then they walk away.

One subtle fact seems to go unnoticed: the fact that my *staring* went unnoticed by everyone. And returned by no one.

Even when I shower, no one sees me. I'm literally a floor tile in this place. Or a lighting fixture. Or a showerhead. I stand under the spray of hot water, surrounded by naked bodies, slick muscles, and soapy chests through a veil of steam, and not one eye meets mine. I almost make eye contact with a guy across from me, then realize he's checking out the dude to my left.

Just when I decide enough is enough and start drying off, some guy shoves into me on his way out, causing me to stumble under a showerhead, soaking me (and my towel) anew. And as I open my mouth to apologize for being in the way, he grunts, "Watch where you're standing, dipshit," over his thick shoulder before he, his chiseled jaw, and firm model-boy ass strut away.

What a weird instinct I've cultivated over the years.

To apologize for being in everyone's way.

After drying off (again) and getting dressed, I head out of the locker room, my backpack over my shoulder, and beeline for the door. My priority is quite suddenly cracking open a beer the second I get home, then browsing the web for something funny to laugh at. Maybe prank videos. Or cute kittens getting into trouble and falling off furniture.

Until I'm stopped by a voice. "Hey, Romeo?"

The voice comes from the young man at the front desk: Danny Chen, a cute, sweet twenty-something my eyes are *very* familiar with, because whenever he's here, no one and nothing else seems to exist. He's always crisply dressed in his uniform athletic polo, its stretchy material pulling across his toned pecs and tucked into a pair of khakis. His dark hair is flipped up in the front and slightly parted, with subtle highlights that complement his warm, honey-brown complexion. He wears a pair of thin, stylish glasses he keeps pushing up with a finger every few minutes, which I find to be one of his most adorable habits. He isn't overly muscular, his frame modest and small, but considering the toned nature of his arms and subtly broad shoulders, I'm fairly sure he makes use of the gym he works at.

And whenever he looks at me, my heart goes funny and my brain twists up like a dishrag, robbing me of the ability to form basic sentences.

Which is why I respond to him with a: "I'm hello, yes?"

Danny squints at me, his face going wrong. "Huh?"

I clear my throat, then approach the front desk. "Sorry. Long day. Hello."

"Hey, Romeo." He smiles, showing the tiniest dimples at the corners of his soft, velvety lips—or at least I imagine they're velvety, from all the fantasies I've had about kissing them. "Your membership is about to expire in a few days, and I just wanted to check if—"

"Sure, I'll renew."

"Really? Awesome." He goes to the computer and starts typing, then frowns. "Wish they'd update the system here. Last gym I worked at, all of this would be online or automated and I wouldn't have to bug you."

I prop my elbows on the counter. "Struggles of a privately-owned gym, I guess?"

"You got it."

My gaze dances down from his pretty, deep brown eyes to his tight polo shirt, the gym logo printed on it, right next to his shiny nametag: Danny Chen.

Danny is a nice guy. A real one. The exact kind I'd swipe right on—even if I knew there was no chance of him swiping right back. A guy I'd happily take on a date, hang out with for hours, laugh at each other's jokes, and cuddle with while watching a movie neither of us are really paying attention to, our hearts too distracted as they drum with anticipation.

He's the kind of nice guy where your happiest days aren't even sexual. They're emotional, sweet, and meaningful. They're the mug of hot cocoa by a fire, and the blanket he thoughtfully wraps you in. They're holding each other in a cushy old armchair that smells like every holiday season, me stroking his arm thoughtfully while telling him about my day. They're us at a rescue shelter, picking out which sweet puppy to take home, and choosing what we'll name him or her.

He's the guy who makes it easy to believe in a happy-ever-after.

I can imagine it all with Danny, as if our life is a beautiful memory I haven't made yet.

"You're all set," he announces with another breath-stealing smile. "Membership renewed."

And despite all my doubts, I might even have the courage to ask Danny on a date, if it weren't for one stinging, unfortunate setback.

3. The Setback

"DUDE!" BOOMS THE SWEATY, MUSCLED MONSTER FROM behind, marching from the weight machines up to the front counter. "Danny, what the fuck, babe? The staff aren't cleaning the machines! I just sat down in a puddle of some old man's sweat on the chest press."

The setback is an obnoxious, entitled, amateur bodybuilder named Joey.

Danny's *jerk* of a boyfriend.

Joey has upper-body muscles for days, but they seem out of proportion with his skinny legs, like he spends all his time in the gym doing angry bicep curls and nothing else. (Except eating small children for protein, maybe.) Though he might have a handsome face, he always seems to be scowling, no matter his mood. He has a tanned complexion that turns angry and rosier at his cheeks, and a head of bleached blond hair that always appears gelled so solidly in place, it looks like a yellow Lego hairpiece.

"Ugh, I'm sorry," says Danny. "I'll get someone on it. We're short-staffed, since Brian pulled a muscle and had to take the day off."

Joey crosses his big arms, slick with sweat, and rolls his eyes. "Yeah, probably a lie so he can stay home and pull *another* muscle all day long, the horny loser." He doesn't even acknowledge that I'm standing right next to him. I literally don't exist. "If you're short-staffed, you should put up a sign or something. 'Clean up after your sets. Wipe off the machines. Don't be a filthy pig.' It isn't rock science."

I think he means rocket science, but apparently Danny is too nice to correct him. "You've got a great point, babe."

"I know." Joey scoffs. "This place doesn't clean itself, obviously. Hey, and you're out of towels, too."

"I'll get Desiree on it."

Without even so much as a thank-you, Joey pushes away from the counter and goes back to the machines. Danny smiles after him, then lets out a tiny sigh and faces me. "Sounds like I've got some work to do. Thanks for renewing your membership, Romeo."

I keep wanting to say it's just Rome, but something about the formality and respect he gives my full name every time he utters it keeps me from telling him. Maybe I like it. I smile back and prepare to thank him—when a loud *clang* from Joey dropping his weight after a deadlift distracts us both.

"Guess I better get on those towels before my boyfriend breaks the floor," says Danny before excusing himself from the front desk, leaving me on my own.

I'm not sure what comes over me. Maybe it's the way he looks when he walks away like he's on a mission. Or it's the lingering emotion that twists up in my chest like a restless balloon animal. Or that spark of insanity that often accompanies intense feelings for someone you know you can't have.

But the next moment, I'm hurrying to his side. "I can help."

Danny blinks at me, then chuckles. "Why? Are you looking for a new job or something?"

"Nope. But you did say you're short-staffed, and everyone deserves to have ... uh ... towels and sweat-free workout benches."

The cutest smile spills over his face. "You're right about that, Romeo." He pokes his head through a door leading into a back room, where I hear the hum of laundry machines. "Hey, Desiree? Can you get some more towels? We're out. Thanks." He lets the door shut, then eyes me. "My boyfriend should be thankful our laundry machines are up and running this week at all, otherwise we'd have *no* towel service. Last Thursday, I swear the dryer was possessed."

"Your boyfriend seems ..." I suddenly realize I can't finish that sentence without sounding rude.

Danny chuckles. "It's okay, you can say it."

"No, no. I wasn't going to, uh, say anything bad. I was just ..." Again, I remain awkwardly silent.

He smirks at me. "You're a bad liar."

I blush.

He takes us to a closet, the door of which seems heavy as he shoves it open. His bicep flexes with the effort, his arms stretching the sleeves of his tight polo. After he's gathered what we need from the back—which I volunteer to carry—he holds the heavy door open for me and says, "You first."

I smile, then start to pass by. The stubborn, heavy door gives a little, causing Danny to scoot forward unintentionally right as I squeeze by, making my passage a tight one—and bringing us into surprisingly close proximity. For one blissful second, we are so close, I feel like I'm in his arms. Everything is slow motion. Danny's beautiful face is in front of mine, gazing at me with his sweet eyes. My hands are filled with sanitizer spray bottles and disinfectant wipes, my heart is in my throat, and our eyes are locked.

The moment ends as fast as it came, and off I go to help Danny wipe sweat off of machines.

Why is a guy like Danny with a guy like Joey? That's all I can think about as I'm wiping down the seat of a leg press machine, sneaking glances at Danny across the aisle and growing more confused by the second. Danny is a one in a million. An angel. A specimen of perfection.

And Joey is a fucking—"You don't have to do this."

I look up. Danny just finished wiping the bicep curl machine. You know, the one Joey probably lives at for two hours a day minimum. "I don't mind helping," I insist.

"Really." He comes up to the fly machine I'm at and starts cleaning the other arm. "*We're* the ones who are supposed to be keeping this place clean. And normally Brian would be out here on the floor looking after things, but—"

"Pulled muscle. I heard. I'm sorry you're left taking up the slack."

"Thanks. And it isn't the first time, either, but I still get the blame. And the added stresses."

"At least you're not dealing with it alone," I add with a smile.

"Hey, you're right! I'm not." He gazes at me, for a moment lost in my eyes. "What a strange feeling."

My smile drops. His tone changed, too. "What's strange?"

"Actually being listened to."

I stop wiping whatever it is I'm wiping, my task forgotten completely.

He smiles at me from across the machine.

I smile back, my heart racing.

Our faces are mere inches apart, separated only by the freshly-wiped-down seat.

Are we having a moment?

Danny glances toward the front desk suddenly. "Phone's ringing." He pushes his glasses back up into place—that adorable habit of his—then shoots me an apologetic smile. "I'll be right back. Our answering machines are down, so I can't let it go, and ... sounds like Desiree can't hear it. I wonder if she even got the towels." He lets out a chuckling sigh. "Are you questioning your decision to renew your membership here yet? It's like it's still 1995 in this place. Answering machines ... Outdated systems ... Phones ... Oh, right, the phone."

He hurries off. I watch him go while gnawing anxiously on my lip. A swirl of excitement, uncertainty, and something else stirs around inside my chest—something I can't name. It's probably heartache. Or horniness.

Sometimes, they feel the same.

It's always like this, isn't it? The guys you want, you can't have. Whether they're straight, taken, or just plain not interested, all the guys you want are off-limits. The only place you can have them is in your dreams, where you feel only half of everything while your eyes are closed, and a whole lot of nothing when you wake up.

A loud thump startles me, and I notice Joey having plopped down at a nearby machine we just cleaned. He grunts demonstratively with every rep, making sure all within earshot are aware of his efforts. He's so much bigger in his head than he is in reality, and it shows in his greedy eyes, in the way he gnashes his teeth when he concentrates, and in how his knuckles turn white with his fierce grip of the machine. Then he finishes, huffing, and leaves the machine without cleaning it.

My imaginary cat ears fold back, annoyed.

What does Danny possibly see in a guy like that?

"Thanks so much for helping out, Romeo," Danny calls out to me as I head for the door, the phone tucked between his shoulder and neck. "I'll see you tomorrow!"

"See you," I say back, then quietly head out.

But it's a lot sooner than tomorrow that I see Danny.

That night as I cuddle under my sheets, ready for bed, I can't get Danny out of my mind. For some reason, I keep hearing the grunting and slamming down of weights, and I can't help but wonder if that's what Danny sounds like when he works out. I can picture him in a pair of tight compression shorts, a matching super-tight sleeveless athletic top, sporty socks, and athletic shoes. He's lying back on a workout bench and grunting as he works out. I'm sure pushing that barbell over his chest again and again is nearly effortless for him. With all of his strength and limitless virility, it's no surprise. Yet his muscles bulge and tighten from the efforts, drawing my eyes and making my heart gallop excitedly.

His skin is glossy from sweat. His scent is irrationally clean and inviting. *Intoxicating, even.*

I throw my bed sheets off, reach into my nightstand, pump some lube into my hand, then free the beast that is my now raging-hard cock. My hand wraps around it, feeling its firm yet silky-soft skin, now slick, and I start to stroke it.

It's incredible, how sensitive my cock gets when I'm so into my fantasy that I feel like I'm imagining something that really happened.

Something that *could* happen.

I don't know where I physically am yet in this fantasy, except that I can see every inch of Danny perfectly, from his shapely calves, to his tight thighs, to his veiny arms, to his tightened face as he grimaces with each rep.

It's devastating, how badly I want him.

My jerking speeds up. My cock responds, flexing and throbbing in my hand.

It's not going to take long.

Then I discover exactly where I am in this fantasy: I'm straddling him as he works out. He either doesn't notice me, or doesn't mind that I'm now sitting on his lap as he continues doing bench presses on his back.

I realize his dick is getting hard in those tight shorts of his, with my ass pressed against it.

Maybe he *does* know I'm here.

As I jerk off, my free hand touches his firm, tight abs, feeling them flex, like moving granite. My hungry fingers slide up the smooth material of his sleeveless shirt, then cup one of his meaty pecs as it swells with every push and lift of the barbell over his chest. He must enjoy the way I'm greedily feeling him up, because now with each rep, he lingers at the top before bringing the barbell back down, as if to show off how strong he is, how puffed up his chest can get, and how he never tires.

His dick throbs against my ass, pushing against it. I start to move my hips as I jerk off, encouraging him. He rocks his eyes back and moans as he continues pushing that weight, determined to finish his set—before one of *us* finishes.

His confidence is so fucking hot.

Is this an exotic gym-boy precursor to how it will be when we have sex?

Will he show off in bed, too? Will he puff up his chest and make me his completely?

Will he never tire, going long into the night, sweaty, glistening, grunting?

I'm close, jerking off with unending desperation. He grunts and flexes and pushes the weights harder now. I feel my insides swiftly coming undone as my hand slides up and down the smooth, silky skin of my achingly hard cock. His dick pushes against the confines of his tight shorts and my gyrating ass, throbbing, tormented. His muscles struggle for the first time as he bites his lip and his breaths become vocal, nearly reaching the end of his set. I bite my own lip, reaching the end of mine.

"Auugh!" Danny growls out as he pushes that weight with all he's got, just to finish that one last rep.

"Mmmph!" I cry out, racing toward the edge, urgent and happy.

Then without warning, I erupt. The fantasy vanishes at once as I unload wave after wave into my other hand, and I moan out with delirious, head-spinning pleasure. When I finish, shockwaves of delight bounce around inside of me, and I smile into the darkness of my room, relieved.

I feel so undeservedly happy right now.

After I clean up, sense returns to me, and I find myself sitting at my small table by the window, naked and pensive, unable to sleep. Thoughts of the totally untouchable, unavailable Danny are far away—as far away as I can push them, at least. I drum fingers against my chin as I give a long, hard look at my dating profile pic on my phone. When I finally decide to replace it with a new one, it isn't the lame cardigan pic Prisha insisted I use. Instead, I choose a smirking selfie I took earlier in the gym bathroom. Sweat drips down my face. My hair is a cute mess. I look like I'm ready for someone to finally take me off this dating app for good. Then I set my phone down and smile at a sputtering streetlamp outside the window, satisfied with myself.

It's in the morning after I've poured myself a cup of orange juice and taken my first bite of a cream-cheese-smeared bagel that my phone dings with a surprising notification.

Someone swiped right.

4. Swipe Right

"YEAH, OKAY, HE *IS* CUTE, BUT—"

I stop Prisha right there. "We have a *lot* in common, too."

"But just because *someone* swipes right doesn't mean—"

"Look, he's into reading high-fantasy fiction, video games, Dungeons & Dragons, and loves watching anime. Literally *no one* that cute admits that in a dating profile if they're just looking for a hookup."

"You said that about your last date, and then he seemed a lot more interested in eating out your ass than rolling high dice on a fireball spell."

Yes, I tell Prisha everything—even that. "I know, but this is different."

"You always say that, too." She kicks back the last of her beer, then slaps down her cup on the end table next to her. Dakota's party started out loud and has only gotten louder. The apartment is crowded. We've found the only space we can breathe is in the corner of the room by the opened window, the sill of which I'm sitting on, with a clear view of the front door if we decide to bounce. "But the day after your

26

date, which will inevitably turn out horribly, I know exactly what I'll be doing. Consoling you. Drinking sparkling rosé with you. Looking for a Twilight marathon on TV."

"Twilight mara—?"

"And as much as I love a nice rosé, my dear Rome, I'd rather be drinking one with you to *celebrate* something. Not to drown out your tears."

"His last message to me was asking if I wanted to meet up for a movie. Should I say yes? I haven't replied yet."

She lets out a sigh. "Isn't there anyone you've got your eye on who *isn't* at the other end of a two-and-one-quarter-star-rated dating app?"

Just then, the apartment door opens with a new arrival to the party.

Danny.

I watch him through cracks in the crowd, my breath held. He greets someone, laughs at something, then points off somewhere, maybe asking where the drinks are. When he turns to go, his boyfriend Joey enters the apartment, too, and though he isn't wearing his usual scowl, the bodybuilding loser already looks two or three drinks in, his eyes watery and happy as he follows Danny to the kitchen.

"Rome?"

I turn back to Prisha. "Sorry, what?"

"I asked if you've got your eye on anyone."

"I ..."

"Yes?"

My arms fold over my chest. Okay, I tell Prisha *almost* everything. "I guess I *do* have a little crush on someone."

27

"A little crush? What are we? In middle school?"

I wonder what Danny is doing here. Does he know Dakota? How else did he get invited? "Hey, you asked if I have my eye on anyone, and yes, I do."

"So who is it?"

"It doesn't matter." I gaze off toward the kitchen with a smirk. "He's with someone anyway."

Prisha sighs and is about to say something when Juan, a coworker of ours, appears out of nowhere and shouts: "Hey, Prisha! I gotta talk to you about a thing!"

She nods. "I'll be right there!" Then she eyes me. "I sometimes hate going to these parties. It's like we're all still at work. Hey, by the way, we should have another game night soon. I'm still a bit raw from that last game of Clue we played."

I roll my eyes. "I'm telling you, I did *not* cheat."

"Yet somehow knew it was Miss Scarlet in the kitchen with the lead pipe after just two clues."

"It's *always* Miss Scarlet. That lady is shady as fuck."

She smirks. "I'm going to go talk to Juan. Maybe I can rope him into a game night. Promise you'll be here when I get back and won't bail without me?"

"Promise."

"Shouldn't be long." And away she goes, disappearing into the crowd.

I stare at the kitchen from across the room, gnawing on my lip. For a second, I was tempted to pull out my phone and see if my swipe-right guy has said anything else after popping the question about hitting up a movie together. Now, all of my focus is stolen by one such cutie from the gym, and my phone is forgotten completely.

So is my promise to Prisha that I'd wait here for her.

I ditch the window and make my way toward the kitchen, gently maneuvering my way through the crowded room. To my surprise, I don't find Danny there. I ease my way through the noisy crowd to the hallway, but he's not there either. I poke a head into a darkened bedroom, but there's just a few people hanging out on the bed watching two guys duke it out on a video game. "Dude, shut the door, you're letting the light in!" someone shouts at me. "Sorry," I mutter, then quickly close the door and frown, wondering where Danny has gone. There are only so many places he can be in this apartment. Is he hiding in an air duct?

Where the hell is he?

As I make my way back through the living room, I realize quite suddenly that the claustrophobia is getting to me. I make a quick beeline for the back window to get a breath of air. I slip a leg through, then let myself out onto the fire escape.

And that's when I find myself face-to-face with Danny.

"Oh," I let out, startled. "I didn't see—"

He lifts his eyebrows. "Hey there, Romeo!"

He's standing out here by himself with a bottle of beer. Tonight, he's wearing a tight-fitting white graphic shirt, clinging to his arms and chest, and tapering down to his small waist, where the shirt is ever so slightly bunched up at his butt. His distressed jeans are doing everything to highlight the asset that *is* his ass, with two firm and distracting cheeks I try not to glue my eyes to. The way the streetlight catches his face and sets his hair ablaze has my heart fluttering like a desperate butterfly caught in a net.

Does he know I was masturbating thinking about him the other night? Can he see it in my eyes, the inappropriately selfish and unhealthy way I long for him? Is there even a speck of a suspicion burning inside of him that I have strong, undeniable feelings for him I shouldn't in any way entertain?

Suddenly, I'm humiliated I was even looking for him. I grimace, then turn back toward the window. "Sorry, I'll leave you be. I was just—"

"Why? It's nice and quiet out here." A police car races down the street below, its siren blaring. "Quiet-*er*," he amends, pushing at the frames of his glasses. "Stay on the fire escape with me. Keep me company."

I cling to the edge of the sill, take a breath, then decide to oblige him. After all, he's invited me now, right? Doesn't that make it okay? "I guess I can hang out here for a bit."

"Good. Besides, I just got here, and ... I don't really know a lot of people. I'm only here because Joey is loosely acquainted with, um ... what's her name? The one hosting the party?"

"Dakota."

"Right, Dakota." He smiles. "It's good to see *someone* I know, though!"

Someone he knows. Those words put an unexpected warm spot in the cold dead center of my chest. I smile back, then take a place next to him by the railing. My heart is drumming down my arms and up my neck at the same time somehow. "It's great to see you, too."

"Parties are really more Joey's thing. But ... well ... I can't really say no to him when he wants to go out on a Saturday night. Even if all I wanted to do was stay in, relax, and start the next season of *Demon Slayer* after my hard week at work, but ..." Danny lets out a chuckle, though I hear a note of frustration. "I gotta keep my guy happy, right?"

But what about your needs, Danny? What about you? "I guess so."

"Do you have a guy, Romeo?"

I meet his eyes, caught off-guard by the question. I don't ever remember telling him I'm gay. Maybe he's fishing. "Me?" I can't help but laugh. "No."

"No?" Panic fills his eyes. "Oh! Did I misread you? Are you straight? Sorry!"

"No, no. I'm ..." His reaction just makes me laugh harder. *I'm so damned awkward around him.* "I'm definitely into guys. You got that part right."

"Ah, phew! You had me there for a second!" He chuckles adorably. "I'm only asking because you seem like a good catch."

I choke on my laughter, go silent, and lift my eyebrows. "I'm a what?"

He must think I didn't hear him, because he scoots closer. Our arms touch, resting on the railing. "A good catch, I said. I'm just curious why you don't have a guy of your own."

I want to touch him so badly. Other than our arms grazing, I mean. "Guess I've got bad luck in the dating world or something."

"Hmm. Sorry to hear it." Danny studies me for a moment, and I feel like he's stripping away all my thoughts, secrets, and clothes with his soft eyes. Then he shakes his head in pity. "I really hope that luck changes for you, Romeo. Everyone deserves someone to share the world with."

He melts me. With every fucking word he utters, he converts me into a puddle. "Thank you, Danny."

"Hey, this part of town is full of gay men. Not to mention the gym, I'm sure you've noticed. You're bound to meet a great guy who deserves you."

I'm captured by his gaze, dumbstruck.

I can't seem to make words come out of my throat.

Can we just not talk at all? Can I just stand here and stare at him like some drooling, lovesick puppy?

The moment I open my mouth to reply, the window is eclipsed by a big blocky shape that could only be one thing in the known universe. "Babe, the fuck you doing out here? Smells like dog piss."

Danny, sweet as ever, lifts his beer to him. "Just enjoying a drink with my friend Romeo."

Joey glances at me. It may be the first time he's ever acknowledged my existence. Then he turns back to Danny without even a hello. "Let's get outta here. The boys are meeting up at King's for a few drinks. Quick is DJ-ing."

"Haven't you had enough already?"

Joey scoffs. "Yeah, whatever, mommy. I'll wait at the door." He slips back into the apartment.

Danny meets my surprised gaze, then shrugs. "He's a bit to handle sometimes, but I love the guy. You know how it is."

He gives my shoulder a nudge. "You'll understand that soon enough when you've got one of your own! Someone out there is waiting for you, someone amazing."

"I hope so."

He goes for the window, then lingers as he gazes back at me. "See you around, Romeo." Then my eyes snap to his cute butt as he hops through the window and disappears into the crowd inside, leaving me on the fire escape with the late-night noises of the city—and my thoughts.

And after a glance at his cute butt, my thoughts are nothing good right now.

I pull my phone out and bring up the guy who swiped right on my profile, then study his face with a mounting sense of determination.

"Yeah," I say out loud, narrating my reply as my thumbs tap out the words. "Let's meet up for a movie."

5. Popcorny

HE'S OVER TWENTY MINUTES LATE.

I don't mind. I'm not that thrilled about the movie of choice—a zombie thriller with an eye-roll of a title I've already forgotten—so I'm content to just hang out in the lobby until he arrives. Also, it's Sunday afternoon, I have work in the morning, and I had no other plans.

In the meantime, I text back and forth with Prisha, who is busy planning out her game night she can't wait to host. The only two roped into the plans so far are Juan from the office and Prisha's neighbor Marissa. A game of Monopoly is on the itinerary. Also a rematch of Clue, assuming we can even get to it. She also mentioned a round of charades or Pictionary to start with for a "quick warm-up", both of which are Prisha's favorites to play with me since we practically read each other's minds. I'm not sure how late she plans this game night to go considering it's on a Thursday, but Fridays tend to be a blow-off day at the office anyway.

"Rome, sir?"

Sir ...? I turn around, expecting to find one of the movie theater ushers, dolled up in a bowtie and vest, perhaps handing me something I dropped.

Instead, I see my date: skinny, tall, pale except for his flushed red cheeks with an exorbitant amount of freckles, bright coppery-red hair, wearing a Nintendo t-shirt tucked into a pair of low-hanging black slacks with a belt, and a large pair of glasses resting on his nose. Is he going for casual or dressy? Twenty-six years old, yet still looks like a freshman in college. His eyes are bright and eager, like my existence just made him the happiest boy on Earth.

And ... fuck, I completely forgot his name. "Hey there," I vaguely greet my date.

"It's a pleasure to meet you." Then his face collapses. "I'm so sorry I'm late. It won't happen again."

It's like I'm his boss and he just disappointed me on his first day of employment. "Oh, it's okay. I was just—"

"Really, it's fine if you're displeased with me in any way. I'll make it up to you. Have you gotten the popcorn? I'll get you some popcorn." He hurries to the counter of the concession stand behind me as I stare after him, bewildered. "Hi, thanks, I'd like a large popcorn," he tells the bowtie-wearing worker, "for my patient and wonderful date Romeo." He turns back to me. "What's your favorite soda? Can I get you a drink as well?"

"I, uhm ..."

"Will a large Coke appease you?"

Appease me ...? "Sure."

Relief crashes over his face. He turns back to the worker. "A large Coke, please."

I can't say I'm used to being so "served" on a date. Is this what our life would be like, if I continue to date this guy and things got serious? Breakfast in bed every morning. Him cooking me dinner every night and laying a napkin over my lap before I eat. Shoulder massages and chocolates on Valentine's Day and a thoughtful gift every anniversary.

Perhaps I should remember his name first before I go projecting too far into our hypothetical future.

Benjamin? Benny? Bradley? Brian?

We take a seat in the back of the theater, as the previews are already over and the movie itself has begun. To my surprise, he got the popcorn and drink *solely* for me, not to share. "No, really," he insists, "I got this to make up for my being late. It's all yours. I can hold the popcorn for you if you'd like. Yeah, I'll hold it for you, so it doesn't bother your lap or burden you in any way." He keeps the tub of popcorn in his lap, then eyes me. "Oh. Do you want some now?"

It's a bit overwhelming, his submissiveness to my every apparent need. "Um ... sure. I'll take a handful while it's still hot." I start to reach.

"Would you like me to feed it to you?"

I stop.

Feed it to me ...?

"I don't mean in a weird way," he goes on. "I just ... I want to keep your hands from getting buttery. You know how it is. My hands are super clean. I washed them in the bathroom just before meeting you, because I ... I had to check myself in the mirror. I get ... really nervous before a date. You never know what you're getting yourself into, know what I mean?"

He can say that twice and a half. "Y-Yeah."

"So can I feed some to you? A handful while it's hot?" he asks, a slightly playful lilt in his voice.

I can't say this is the *weirdest* thing that's ever happened on a date, but at least it beats being treated badly. Why not have a guy at my every whim? *When Rome's in Rome ...* "Sure."

Benjamin-Benny-Bradley-Brian smiles, happy, then brings a handful of popcorn to my mouth. After only a split second of awkward misgiving, I let him feed me. Popcorny goodness explodes on my tongue. Perfectly crunchy yet soft. Nutty. Sweet. Salty. Buttery. Before I'm finished with the first mouthful, he's already got another, which I go ahead and accept as well.

Again, not the weirdest thing I've done. I'm open-minded.

But I definitely have a few question marks floating over my head. Other than his name, I mean. "So have you ever fed a guy popcorn before?" I tease, trying to make light of this.

He seems to take it very seriously. "No."

It suddenly occurs to me that my date may be "into" this whole subservient thing a little more than he's letting on. He feeds me another handful. I chew away like this is totally our usual routine. Is it more awkward to find what we're doing weird, or to play it off like I do this all the time? How am I supposed to act right now?

Is he even paying attention to the movie?

Am I?

I decide to go for a casual chat—as if I can make this scene between two total strangers seem totally normal. "So tell me what you're looking for in a guy."

"Hmm." He hesitates with my next handful of popcorn, thinking it over. "I guess I'm looking for someone like you, Rome. We both swiped right. We like similar things. And your pic had a real sense of *strength* about it, like you can be really mean if you want to, so I'd better treat you right. I only mean that in a good way. You go to the gym often?"

I knew it was all about that pic. "Every day after work. I remember you said you like reading fantasy novels?"

"Oh, I *love* fantasy in all its capacities. And roleplaying games, like Dungeons & Dragons. Something amazing happens when you become someone else. You're free to do things you don't normally give yourself permission to do, know what I mean?"

Like feed your date popcorn? "I get it. When I play the occasional Dungeons & Dragons game with my best friend, I can be whoever I want." He feeds me another handful. I might be growing too comfortable with this. "Like a warrior with a big sword, for example."

"Yeah?" He stops feeding me, then lowers his voice and brings his lips close. "Do you ... have a big sword, Rome?"

I look at him, my chewing stopped. "Big ...?"

"It's okay if you're sporting more of a ... *short sword*," he says softly. "Or a dagger, even. I'm not picky. It's what's on the inside that counts." He smiles with wistful eyes, as if that's the most romantic thing he has ever uttered in his life. "Am I wearing glasses in my profile pic? Do you remember?

I hope these big things didn't throw you off—the glasses. I lost my contacts getting ready this morning."

I'm still debating what "weapon" I'm wielding in my pants, assuming that's what he was suggesting. Is it weird that I don't know? "No, they didn't throw me off at all. They look nice. Studious. They fit you."

"Do they? Thanks." He blushes, then lifts his eyebrows. "Are you ready for a sip of Coke?"

Is he going to feed me the straw like an airplane? "Sure thing." He lifts the cup, already wet with condensation, to my lips. I suck from the straw, the fizzy goodness exploding in my mouth. Our eyes are connected the whole time. This totally isn't weird. "Thanks," I say after swallowing. "Tasty."

"Is there anything else you want to know about me?"

Neither of us are paying attention to the muscled man on the big screen being devoured by a trio of hungry zombies right now, his blood-curdling screams filling our ears as heavy metal music plays. There is something about my date that makes me err on the side of honesty. "I gotta confess something."

He lowers the cup and popcorn, worry in his eyes. "What is it?"

"I'm drawing a total blank. I can't remember your name."

After a moment of stunned silence, he bursts into laughter—causing someone several rows ahead of us to glance over their shoulder, even over the heavy metal. "I thought it was something worse! Like you thought I was weird or really *did* have a problem with my glasses!"

"Nope, no problem."

"The last date I went on—*Is that against the rules? Can I talk about a date I went on a few weeks ago?*—he didn't like my glasses. I had to take them off the whole time, and I was *so* blind. I felt like I was dating three of him. Oh, I had also lost my contacts then. Hmm, I lose them often," he realizes aloud.

"Your glasses are totally cool." He still hasn't mentioned his name. "I think you should do whatever it is that makes you the most comfortable."

"Are you sure? I like making others comfortable. If you told me right now that you hated my glasses, I would take them right off." He lifts his eyebrows expectantly. "Really, you can test me. I'll do it."

It's like he wants me to. "Um … I like the glasses, but if you—"

"Really, you can just tell me to get rid of them and I will. Whatever you want, goes. You could even do it for fun if you wanted, just to test me. I deserve to be punished for making you wait and missing the beginning of the movie, anyway." He gives me a coy smile, his eyes oddly excited.

"The traffic was pretty bad," I point out. "I can't fault you for that. Besides—"

"You said you live nearby. Did you walk all the way here?"

Boy, this guy shifts gears fast. "I, uh, yes, I did."

"Your feet must be sore. Oh, I have an idea! Let me give you a foot rub."

I blink. "A f-foot rub …? In a movie theater …?"

"Sure, it's no big deal. I'd be happy to do it. That'll make up for my being late. And since you don't want to test telling me to take off my glasses, I'll do this for you instead. How's that sound?"

I have no idea what to make of this. "You still haven't told me your name."

"To be fair, I did, but you forgot," he points out teasingly. Then his face turns serious at once. "But you can call me whatever you want, sir. Call me your personal bitch if it pleases you." He lets out a little laugh, which he quickly swallows as he sets aside the popcorn and drink, drops to his knees, and proceeds to take off my shoes.

And I stare down at him, completely dumbfounded, as he starts to rub my socked feet, digging his thumbs into the soles.

And as weird as this date has gotten, I can't deny how good that feels. "Wow." The word escapes my lips without my meaning it to.

He takes it for encouragement. "You like how I'm massaging them? Feel free to be as critical as you want. Tell me to do better. Or rub harder. You can even tell me to kiss them, if it isn't going too far."

You mean we haven't gone too far already? "I, uh ..."

"You can still tell me to take off my glasses, by the way. Seriously. Or insult my hairdo. Or anything that makes you feel good. Push me around. Call me a nerd. Roleplay as the bully or the jock, if you want. Be a total ... a total *jerk*. I deserve it," he adds with a smile, then rubs my feet with more vigor.

Zombies rampage a supermarket. Firearms are ringing

out on the screen. A man screams and hides behind the counter while a muscled woman in a torn tank top bites the pin off a grenade and throws it into aisle six.

And in row fifteen, a guy whose name I still don't know makes love to my feet.

I bite my lip, uncertain. With a glance at my phone, I notice a ten-minute-old text from Prisha asking me how my date's going and whether I need a fake emergency to escape it.

Then suddenly I feel his face in my crotch.

I move my phone to find him nuzzling my junk with his nose, his eyes rocked back, looking like he's just found heaven.

"H-Hey!" I manage to say, completely taken aback. "I didn't—!"

"Oh." He pulls away, alarmed. "Did I go too far? I thought you'd like it."

What in the hell did I get myself into? "I just didn't think we'd—"

"I really want to pull out your cock and suck it right now. While I'm down here on my knees, with your feet in my lap, my head between your legs. Please, sir, let me do this for you. I'm begging you. I want to make you feel so good. You can pull on my hair if you want. I like it."

I catch myself wondering suddenly how this date would have gone had Danny come to a movie with me instead. Somehow, I can't picture it going in this direction at all. He'd actually watch the movie. He would jump at all the surprise moments when a zombie pops out of nowhere. He would clutch my arm and gasp, then laugh at his own jumpiness.

He wouldn't be on his knees on that sticky floor, begging to give me a blowjob.

And to pull his hair.

And who knows what other clever ideas are in Benjamin-Benny-Bradley-Brian's head.

"I, uh …" I clear my throat. "I don't mean to disappoint you. And I'm definitely not meaning to kink-shame you or anything. I like to think of myself as … as a pretty open-minded guy. In a certain state of mind, I might even be open to this … power-play dynamic you want. But this isn't what I'm looking for." I grimace. "I really just wanted to have a nice date, get to know you, and enjoy a movie together."

"A … A nice date …?"

"Yeah."

"Oh." He settles back on his heels, then adjusts his glasses, which have gone slightly askew.

I frown. Maybe I'm going about this wrong. To be fair, I've never held an honest conversation with someone whose face is an inch from my crotch. "Did I disappoint you?"

"I'm not into conventional sex," he admits, then looks up at me. "And since we had a lot in common from our profiles, I thought you'd be the kind of guy who's open to new experiences. But I think I pushed my fantasy onto you too strongly. I projected my own desires without reading yours. I guess that's on me." He keeps holding my feet, unsure what to do with them.

He is surprisingly thoughtful and introspective for someone who's only desire was to bow down and blow me a second ago. Something tells me there's more about him than meets the eye.

Still, I consider my phone. I still have the freedom to pretend an emergency came up with my bestie. It's not too late to take hold of that rope Prisha threw me.

"I guess a blowjob is still out of the question?" he asks.

I stare down at him. "I'm so sorry. I'm not really into hooking up like this."

"I see."

"I'm sorry." Why do I keep apologizing? "I really am." *Still apologizing.* "I'll pay for the popcorn and the drink. You didn't have any of either."

"It's okay. I liked doing that for you. I'm kinda into that, too—spending money on others." He adjusts his glasses. "Can I, uh … still rub your feet, though? Just a friendly foot rub?"

Considering how happy it makes the guy, it seems almost cruel to deny him. I give one last glance at my phone, then pocket it and shrug. "Okay, if you really want to. A little harder at the heels, maybe?"

His eyes light up. "Yes, sir."

6. *Open Minds*

ANOTHER VERY LONG MONDAY AT THE OFFICE HAS ME AND Prisha exhausted beyond words, despite the help Juan gave our team in coining a catchy tagline for an ad we're developing. With everyone else bailing out of our usual workout plans, Prisha and I spend an hour downstairs on the treadmills alone, having ourselves a "spirited jog" to blow off some steam.

It's evident from her silence that she's refraining from giving me a "told you so" speech about my recent date—which tied up rather quickly after the movie was over, and not in a kinky way. All Prisha asked me this morning when we got to the office was how last night went, I answered with a shrug, and that was it.

I guess that shrug said it all.

When we're grabbing our stuff to go, she turns to me. "Hey, don't forget about our game night after work on Thursday. My parents are coming into town for the weekend, so … knowing them … I'll be occupied from Friday through the last possible second on Sunday."

"Oh, this weekend is your parents already? I thought that wasn't for another month. Is your mom making some of her famous—?"

"Yes," Prisha cuts me off, "and I'll get you as much of her special Tandoori chicken as I can. I'd say you can come over and get it yourself—*she misses and adores you*—but then she'd never let you leave."

"True. Also, she'd probably ask whether I have a girlfriend yet."

"And why it isn't me. Yes, I know."

Just as we reach the door, I spot Danny at the front counter talking on the phone while typing into the computer. Everything is lost for a moment as I stare at him, curious whether it's a good idea or not to strike up a conversation today. I noticed earlier that Joey isn't here.

"Debating staying for a shower again?" asks Prisha rather dryly.

I eye her. "I don't like that tone and all the dirty stuff you're suggesting with it."

She shakes her head. "I'll see you tomorrow then. Be safe." And off she goes, seeing herself out.

After taking a breath and coaching myself to play it cool, I slowly approach the front desk. Danny spots me right away, gives me a cheery smile, then seems to finish up rather quickly with his phone call, hanging up. "Romeo! How was your workout?"

I'm totally loving how attentive and smart he looks in his tight polo today. "It's really more like a therapy session with my music playlist than an actual workout," I admit.

"You'd be surprised how many people use the gym as a solo therapy session."

"But it was great anyway. Cleared my head. Helped me get past my ... strange Sunday."

"Strange Sunday?" Danny folds his arms on the counter and leans forward, curious.

Well, I just kicked that door wide open, now didn't I? "I went on a movie date with a guy."

His eyes light up. "Oh! That's awesome!" Then he squints and pushes at his glasses. "Hmm. I'm gathering from your tone that it didn't go well ...?"

"It turns out he ... had some special interests I couldn't quite fulfill. He wanted me to talk down to him and rough him around. Dom stuff, I guess. Also wanted me to call him my little bitch and kept asking me to be meaner to him. He even wanted me to spit on his face while he rubbed my feet."

"Wow, that sounds ... less than boring."

"So I guess I wasn't the guy he was looking for. And he agreed after the movie, told me he thought I 'wasn't assertive enough'. He needed—and I quote—a 'real, cocky, badass douchebag to own the shit out of him'. He didn't mention that part in his dating profile. Or else I clearly overlooked it." I shrug. "I hope he finds his Prince Charming ... or in this case, his Prince Douche. Either way, it's not me." I lean in and bring down my voice. "He, um, also wanted to blow me right there in the theater, but—"

"Wait. Really??"

"I wasn't about to take advantage of the poor guy. Especially since I knew by that point that I wasn't what he wanted. It just isn't right, you know what I mean?"

A smile touches his eyes. "That's rather noble of you."

I lift an eyebrow. "It is?"

"Yeah. It really is. Most of the guys I know would've gone for the easy lay, no matter what. Or let him blow them, just to get sucked off." He wags a finger teasingly at me. "I knew there was something special about you, Romeo. You don't play around with guys' hearts. You're one of the nice ones."

The nice ones. "I am?"

"Of course you are." He smacks me on the arm and laughs. "Don't act like it's such a huge surprise. You know you have a good heart. It's obvious."

Would it still be so obvious if he knew how badly I lusted for him? If he knew what I really thought of his boyfriend Joey? If he knew that I'd leap at any chance to be close to him, even if it was wrong?

"Thank you, Danny."

He also leans forward on the counter, bringing our faces close. "I'm just saying the truth. Though I'm also sorry the date didn't turn out well in the end. Don't be discouraged."

I gaze into Danny's sweet eyes. "Hey, at least I got a free foot rub out of it."

He chuckles. *I love the way he laughs.* "And so your bad luck streak continues."

I smile appreciatively. I love that he remembers little details of our conversations like that. "The bad luck streak continues, indeed."

Just then, a loud bang of a weight dropping startles me. I

turn to find two gorgeous, muscled men at the bench press, one of them spotting the other. At first I just assume they're a pair of friends, until the one on the bench gets up and gives the other a kiss on the lips. They smile, slap each other's backs, then go for another set.

I sigh wistfully, watching them. "I guess I just gotta hold out for ... something like *that* to drop into my lap."

"Looks can be deceiving, you know."

I turn back to Danny to find him frowning, gazing at them, too. "What do you mean?"

"Not everyone is as happy as they look on the outside. Not every 'perfect' thing you see is ... perfect."

My lips part. Is he about to tell me how unhappy he is? Is this the moment of truth?

"And the more you romanticize guys like that," he goes on, "the more you forget that they are human beings, too. They get moody. They get needy. They throw tantrums, or smell weird, or have annoying habits."

Does Joey smell weird? Does Joey have annoying habits? "I guess you're right."

"Maybe." He smiles as his eyes return to mine. "I just think everyone's always chasing this idea of a 'perfect guy', like they have any idea what he actually looks like or who he is. But who *really* knows what will make us truly, lastingly happy?" Danny shakes his head and shrugs. "It isn't always what we think. Or *who* we think."

Tell me you're unhappy. Tell me you want more than Joey. Please. "Yeah?"

"We have to keep an open mind about it. Embrace all the

possibilities, and—" The desk phone rings. "Sorry, one sec."

When he pulls away from me to get the phone, I feel a vacuum in my heart, desperate for him to just finish his point and confess how miserable he is with Joey. I'm literally glued to the front of this damned desk, resenting it for being in the way.

"Jesse's Fitness. This is Danny Chen. How can I—? No, I'm sorry, Desiree isn't in today. No, I'm afraid we don't offer classes for—Oh, sure, I can connect you with Louis if you—Oh, okay, no prob, I can sign you up. Can you provide me your full name or email so I can look up your membership?"

I'm a terrible person, I've just decided.

I can't keep rooting for the end of his relationship. I can't keep doing this to myself, either. I shouldn't even be standing at this counter. No matter how horrible of a human being Joey might be, I can't act like it's my purpose in life to see their end, then snatch up Danny for my own.

What kind of person is my own desperation turning me into?

"Desiree will be in tomorrow," says Danny, smiling. "Sure, thanks, have a great evening!" He hangs up, then squints at me. "Sorry about that."

"It's okay. I probably shouldn't be taking up your time or distracting you from—"

"Oh, you're not distracting me or taking up anything." He returns immediately to his position leaning over the counter, right where I can nearly feel the warmth coming off his body. *I don't deserve that warmth.* "I like talking to you, Romeo."

Fuck me.

My heart peels off all its clothes and melts into a puddle of giggles right there from his words.

What am I supposed to do with that?

"So, uh ..." Danny clears his throat and squints at me. "What was I talking about before—?"

"You were telling me I should keep an open mind."

"Right! Keep an open mind and an open heart. To everything. I mean, look at me. I never thought in a million years I'd be with a guy like Joey, and now we're going on two years."

Two years? I can't believe they've been together that long. How did it start? What did Joey do or say to convince Danny to be his boyfriend? And was it done at gunpoint?

"Well, *almost* two years," he says. "Granted, the whole first year, we kinda dragged our feet on officially calling ourselves boyfriends, because he was a bit of a commitment-phobe, but ..." He chuckles and shakes his head. "Sorry, you didn't ask for my life story, *nor* did you ask for my advice. Why do I keep doing this?" He laughs again.

Even his apologies and awkward laughter make me weak in the knees. "I appreciate it anyway," I assure him. "Really, it helps to have your perspective. I have no gay friends, so—"

He gapes. "No gay friends??"

"Just my friend and coworker Prisha. She's technically bi, but kinda hates labels, and has only dated men, except for one short thing in high school apparently, so ... I guess she's the closest thing I have to a gay friend ...?"

"Romeo." His tone drips with mock disapproval. "I can't

believe you have no gay friends. A guy like you? I mean, who do you take as your wingman to the bars or clubs?"

"No one. Prisha, sometimes, but that's just when we want to have fun and let loose."

Danny smacks the counter. "I've got an idea. Call me crazy, but I'm feeling like you and I really have something going on here between us."

You have no idea. "Between us …?"

"Yeah!" He folds his arms on the counter and nods at me. "I'm gonna be your gay friend, Romeo. You can protest all you want, I don't care if I'm pestering you, but this world is just as huge and lonely as it is small and crowded. Us gay guys gotta stick together."

I'm not protesting.

I'm ecstatic.

He and I can stick together as much as he wants.

"Yeah," I finally agree, despite my clambering heart rate due to the sudden proximity of our faces. Of course it'd race *now* and not while I was on the treadmill earlier. "We need to stick together."

"So it's a done deal." Danny nods and smacks the counter again, his bicep bulging and his eyes lighting up in the cutest way. "Next time you go looking for a date, I'm your wingman. I'll be there to support you, to spot the single guys you should go after, and to encourage you. And once you've found your man, I'll disappear and be on standby with my phone. We're going to find you a decent fellow, Romeo!"

I've already found one. He's standing right in front of me, just a tiny desk separating us. "Yeah? Is that what we're gonna do?"

"You bet your ass."

At the sight of his broad, captivating smile—or maybe just his sexy use of the word "ass"—all of my worry and sadness vanishes.

He told me to keep an open mind about happiness.

I hope he's doing the same.

Danny snaps his fingers. "Hey, I just remembered I'm off tomorrow night. Want to hit up a couple of bars? Throw in your figurative fishing line? See what's out there? It'll be fun!"

I don't know if I have it in me to play out this whole wingman thing Danny is proposing.

I don't know if I can trust my own emotions.

Is any part of me really in it to find a guy, or do I just want to spend a night out on the town with Danny, using this whole dating thing as an excuse? *Can't he tell I'm crazy about him? Or is he really that oblivious to his own magnetism?*

7. *Wingman*

OKAY, MAYBE I ALREADY REGRET AGREEING TO THIS.

"Um ... are you *sure* you don't have anything dressier than that?" he asks politely.

I gaze down at my button-up shirt and jeans. I frown at Danny. "What's wrong with this? It's nice."

"Sure, if you're going to church. Do you have anything more ... fitted?" He sucks his tongue in thought, peering up and down my body as he crosses his arms. "Actually, y'know what? A true wingman looks out for his buddy in *every* way. Let's go take a look at your closet together."

"Wait. What?"

"I swear it won't be long." He slaps me on the back and ushers me into my own apartment building.

I don't know why I agreed to meeting him outside my place. Probably because I'm insane, or had some kind of fantasy of this exact thing happening: him coming up to my apartment, then us ditching the idea of going out tonight and deciding to hang out with each other instead.

Wait. Could that still happen? Is it too late?

What the fuck am I thinking?

"Sorry about the place," I say when we arrive. I open the door and let him in. "I didn't expect to, uh, have any company."

"You didn't expect to have company? Were you planning to take your date back to *their* place? I guess you could, but … sometimes, you just don't know where the night will take you. Better to be ready. Here, I'll help you clean up a few things. You don't mind, do you?"

With that—and before I can answer—he proceeds to start fixing up anything he can find: a lopsided throw blanket on the back of my couch, an out of place picture frame, extra crap on my coffee table, a crooked lampshade … It's amazing how many things he finds.

And as he darts around, I can't peel my eyes off of him.

Danny looks delicious tonight. He's wearing a stylish blue dress shirt that seems stitched to fit his every curve, and jeans that make his ass look like a fucking *snack*. Not to mention his bright white shoes, which are commanding and totally fit him. Plus, I guess he's got contacts in for our night out, because he isn't wearing glasses, and that does everything to feature his gorgeous eyes.

And now he's playing housekeeper to my little box of an apartment.

Is this how our life together could be like? Is this a foreshadowing of our future? Is this—

Ugh, this is so wrong.

He stops suddenly. "Let me know if I'm being too …" He bites his lip as he worries over the word. "I don't know. Joey says I can get kind of neurotic. Or controlling. Or something. Hey, do you have a moody lamp you can leave on? A mood-setter?"

"A mood-setter ...?"

"Yeah. You always need to leave at least one lamp on to set the mood. Just in case you bring him back here. It's never good to wander into a dark apartment. So? Do you have one?"

I shrug. "I guess the one by the couch."

He glances at it, flicks it on, then observes it for a moment, drumming his fingers along his chin. His eyes lift up, noticing my plant I keep on the windowsill. "Oh, that looks nice. Definitely a good omen to a potential boyfriend. Shows that you care for something other than yourself." He smiles at me. "That's a good subconscious first impression to send of your lifestyle, know what I mean?"

I chuckle. "If you say so."

"I *do* say so." He walks up to it and tenderly touches some of the leaves, then turns back to me and smiles. "Alright, I think we're set. How about you show me your wardrobe?"

I nod, then lead the way.

This part may take a while.

Half an hour later: "Hmm ..." He thumbs through the limited selection in my closet. "No, not this. No, not this either, sends the wrong message. Hmm, and this one is too casual. Oh, hey, this is kind of nice ... but the material is a bit heavy." He glances back at me. "Sorry, I'm being a handful. But as your only gay friend, I feel like I've got an obligation to be honest."

"You're being great and helpful," I assure him, "and I appreciate it."

"Thanks! Hey, actually, this one is pretty decent." He pulls a shirt off of its hanger. "Pair this with *these*," he says, tugging on a pair of jeans I haven't worn in probably a year, "and maybe we got something going on. Here. Try these on."

He lays the shirt and jeans on the bed next to me.

I stare at him, dumbfounded.

He wants me to change into them. Right now. In front of him.

I'm used to changing in front of guys. I'm not shy in that way. But this isn't the locker room. This is my bedroom. And he's not just any locker room guy; he's Danny Chen, the one person I'm downright infatuated with.

Also, all I'm wearing underneath is a pair of boxer briefs that will show *everything*.

Every *inch* of everything.

"Trust me," he says, "you're gonna look great. I've got an eye for this kind of thing."

He thinks the clothes he picked out for me—from my own closet—are the problem.

Phew.

But I decide to be brave. I have no choice, really. After one last second of hesitation, I kick off my shoes, then unzip and drop my pants. As I unbutton and peel off my shirt, my eyes keep hopping over to Danny for some reason, like they're two nervous, hungry boys who keep jumping from their seats to taste-test everything on the dinner table.

Danny is the scrumptious, meaty, steaming spread.

And I can't get enough.

"You're totally blessed with perfect hair, by the way, so no problem in *that* department."

I stop and face him, down to nothing but my underwear.

I was seconds from grabbing the shirt off the bed, and now he's caught me in another net with his words. "P-Perfect hair ...?"

"Aww, don't be modest now!" He comes right up to me.

Right up to me.

Nearly against me.

In just my underwear.

Then—of all things—Danny proceeds to run his soft, caring fingers through my hair.

I stare into his eyes, paralyzed, melted, and terrified all at once.

"See what I mean?" he says, oblivious to my inner hurricane. "No matter what you do to it, it just sort of ... settles right into place, into a perfect style."

Danny's words swim circles in my ears as I feel electricity in every limb of my exposed, nearly-naked body, from my fingertips to my toes, at the simple combing of his fingers through my hair. His face is right in front of mine, and though his eyes are on my hair that he keeps playing with, I feel hopelessly affixed to him, connected as if by concrete, by diamond, by something impossibly strong and unbreakable.

All of that electricity starts to flood somewhere else.

Somewhere down below my waist.

Oh, no.

He meets my eyes, and a soft smile touches his full, kissable lips. "See?" he says gently. "Your hair is amazing."

I'm at a complete loss. I can't even thank him properly.

More electricity swells and churns down there. Desperate. Excited. Insatiable.

And his fingers keep combing my hair, stroke after curious stroke.

And his smile keeps hovering in front of my face. His adorable smile. His lips I've dreamt of.

His brilliant eyes.

I want this moment and all of these feelings inside me to last forever. This is the exact emotion I've been chasing with every fantasy of mine, with every speck of hope I build for the prospect of a good date, with every squeeze of my pillow at night when I fall asleep alone.

This is it. This is what I want.

Then Danny glances down at once. I do the same, for a moment pulled from my dreams.

Those dreams are replaced with a nightmare: I'm hard as a rock.

Sticking out like an accusatory finger—and pointing right at Danny.

"Oops." His hand stays in my hair. He keeps staring down at it. "I, uh, wow, you're big."

I turn away at once, my face flushing red, as his hand slips from my hair. "Sorry. Um …" I try to laugh it off, but end up just choking on my own breath as I grab the pants off the bed and feverishly begin to thrust my legs into them.

Except the pants are tight.

Very tight.

And my hard dick won't fit in them. "It's, uh … It's been a while since someone's put their hands in my hair and, um, I just, uh …" I keep trying to shove my dick into these jeans. I push one way, it pops out another. I try to bend it, and it aches and flexes against my efforts, determined to stay as stiff as a goddamned plank. "Sorry, I'm having trouble, uh …"

"Hey, it's okay, we're both guys, we're both gay. There's nothing to worry about."

This is more than embarrassing. "I mean, I wasn't expecting to have my hair stroked so much, and I'm just in my underwear, and—"

"It's nice hair!" Danny insists with half a laugh. "That's all I was saying!"

I shut my eyes and try to think of gross things. Or sad things. Or literally anything that'll get my cock to soften. Nothing works. I go back to stuffing it inside, this time with more intent than before, and at last I manage to zip up my jeans—with no regard at all to my comfort. I grab the shirt, quickly throw it on, then sigh as I stare at the bed.

I can't believe all of this just happened.

Could this night start out any worse?

"Come on, turn around," he urges me. "Let's see how you look."

Oh, well. The boner has to go down at some point. I turn around, pretend not to be mortified, and face Danny with a spread of my hands. "Well?"

He gives me a once-over. Then he nods with approval. "I think we're ready to get you a guy."

"Great." I swallow. Yes, I'm still hard. Yes, it sorta shows, even in the jeans. "And, um ... seriously. My ... uh, erection was just a—"

He grips me by the arms suddenly. I freeze and stare at him. "Look, Romeo. If we're going to be friends, we need to be comfortable with stuff like that. It's normal. We're men. Our bodies react. You have nothing to be ashamed of. No apologies, alright? I've seen you at the gym, anyway. And clearly your efforts are paying off."

I blink. "They are?"

"Yeah. You look good in *and* out of your clothes."

This isn't helping my erection. "I do?"

"Oh my god, Romeo, you *have* to know how good you look! Self-confidence is what attracts others to you!" He lowers his voice and turns serious. "Fall in love with the guy in the mirror first before you dare to give your heart to anyone else. That's my motto." He winks at me, slaps my arm, then steps back. "Now are you ready to hit the town with your new gay bestie or what?"

I know I'm falling in love. But it has nothing to do with the guy in the mirror.

8. Buzz

THE PLACE IS LOUD. THE MUSIC IS THUMPING. THE DRINKS are clinking.

And my luck is fast dwindling. Already, we've been here for an hour, and every guy who approaches us only hits on Danny. That's over sixteen men, by the way. Sixteen different, perfectly eligible bachelors all go for the guy who's already taken, and I'm basically a wall ornament.

One tanned hunk in a leather jacket with a stubbly, chiseled jaw put a hand on Danny's back and said, "Hey there, sexy. Can I get you a drink?" And Danny with all his charm only responded: "Nah, I'm just waiting on my boyfriend. But you can buy one for my single man Romeo here!"

He didn't.

Another guy swooped up to Danny's side minutes later— muscled, tight-shirted, smooth glowing skin the color of rich caramel, and a dimpled smile—and said, "What're you doing here all by yourself? Can I join you?" Danny laughed and said, "I'm not by myself. I'm here with my single buddy

Romeo, and he'd totally love your company." The guy put a hand on Danny's thigh—I noticed right away and felt an instant pang of jealousy—but Danny politely brushed it off and said, "I've got a boyfriend, sorry."

The guy didn't keep *either* of us company after that.

The routine carried on and on, with one hottie after another. "Have you met my friend Romeo?" asked Danny yet again. "It blows my mind he isn't taken!"

And yet to someone else: "No, I'm not available, but my adorable buddy Romeo here is! Want to join us for a drink?"

Each time, the potential fish slips away as fast as he can and swims back into the sea. I'm not too broken up about all of the rejection, to be honest. I doubt getting a guy was ever truly the goal. And didn't Danny say I need gay friends? Maybe that's the purpose of all of this instead.

"You know, it's okay," I tell him after a sip—and after the last guy leaves us alone. What am I even drinking? Danny ordered it. "I really don't need to find a guy tonight. I'm having plenty of fun spending time with just you."

Danny is too busy scanning the crowd for my next potential date that he misses the compliment. "Don't give up, buddy. There's plenty of fish here. Oh, I think that guy over there is eyeing us."

We both know he's eyeing only Danny. Or at least *I* do. "Really, I don't mind. I'm sure I can find a hit on my app right now if I really wanted to."

"You should really delete that app."

"Why? At least *those* guys actually show up for a date." I take another sip, then frown in thought, remembering a few dates who stood me up. "Most of the time."

He turns my way and squints at me, as if I just said something either super offensive or super interesting.

Then he snaps his fingers. "You know what? I think I figured it out."

I lift an eyebrow. "Figured what out?"

"The problem. Why you're not catching the right guys. I think you're too much in your head."

"In my head …?"

"I can see it in your eyes," he goes on. "And I think it's why you insist on using dating apps instead of meeting people in the real world."

"Huh? That's not true."

"Dating apps are easier for you, right? You get all the time you need to plan and fine-tune your first impression, hide your flaws, show only a version of you that you want them to see … but guess what? Everyone else does the same thing. And by the time you actually go on a date, neither of you recognize the guy from the profile."

Honestly, I didn't take him for being so brainy about all of this. My head swims with thoughts. Or maybe I'm just buzzed. "Hmm."

"That's why your last date didn't work out," he explains. "Well, judging from your profile pic, at least, which you showed me. You're sweaty, in the gym, looking super tough and dominant. That isn't what you're about, but your date thought it was, so he swiped right. Then all of his fantasy-building from gazing at your profile pic didn't pan out when he met you."

I frown. "So it's my fault?"

"Well, not fully. He did the same thing, didn't he? He should have indicated that he's looking for a dominant type of guy. Or better yet, search on a different dating app altogether that caters to his interests, if he keeps meeting guys who aren't into his thing." Danny takes a sip from his drink.

I gaze at the side of his face. He's so sincere. So analytical. *He just gets deeper and deeper.* "How did you and your boyfriend meet?"

The question throws him off. "Me and Joey? Oh." He sets his hands on the counter. One of them is very close to mine, where I'm gripping my drink. "Well, he and I were … a weird sort of friends-of-friends situation. He was new in town. We had mutual friends at the gym. It was inevitable."

I'm staring at his hand. "Inevitable …?"

"Sure. I mean, I really wanted a boyfriend. I was going through a rough time after my dad died."

I look up at him. He looks so beautiful, even in the dim lighting. "I'm sorry to hear that."

"Thanks. I guess Joey was … exactly the caring kind of guy I needed."

I nearly choke on my own breath. *Caring? That douchebag?* "Wow."

Danny must hear the tone in my voice. "Wow?"

My tongue feels looser. Okay, maybe I *am* buzzed. "I guess I've just … not seen that side of Joey quite yet." I let out a cackle—which was supposed to be just a chuckle. I clear my throat. "I'm surprised, that's all I mean." I go for another sip.

"Surprised about what? How caring Joey can be?" He smiles with amusement. "It is a bit surprising, I know. But underneath that rough exterior, I swear he's a gentle soul, especially when you get to know him. He can—"

I laugh, cutting him off. "Joey comes off as an *awful* human being most of the time." Whoops, I didn't mean to put that so bluntly. How many of these drinks have I had? "Sorry, that came out wrong." I take yet another sip, then rethink it. "Actually, no, it didn't come out wrong. It came out exactly as I meant it. Joey's a ... a fucking *dick*."

For a second, Danny thinks I'm kidding. Then his face tightens and he tilts his head.

And then my heavily-bound flood gates fly open. "He's rude to you at the gym, Danny. I see it. I hear it. He's demanding. He's unkind. I can't even imagine what he's like when it's just the two of you alone."

Danny stiffens up. "He's not *that* bad. He's just a bit ... challenging now and then."

I roll my eyes. "And you call *yourself* an honest person?"

"What do you mean by that?"

"For someone who is so 'honest' all the time, you sure like to do backflips justifying your boyfriend's heinous behavior." I gulp the rest of my drink and slam the glass on the counter a touch harder than I meant to. I guess I misjudged the distance. "I said it already, and I'll say it again: Joey is a fucking dick."

Now Danny is annoyed. "What's gotten into you?"

"I'm just reporting what I see. Joey is *nothing* like you. He isn't caring at all. For all I can tell, you're deeply unhappy with him."

"I'm not unhappy!"

"And I'm supposed to take advice from you on how to find a guy for myself?" I laugh suddenly. "Do you even see what's happening tonight? Everyone wants *you*. Not *me*."

"Romeo."

"And by the way, you're the only person on Earth, apart from my late great grandmother, who calls me by my full name. It's annoying. I go by 'Rome'." I clear my throat. My eyes are super watery, I have to blink to see straight. "Actually, calling me by my full name is adorable, and I kind of like it. And *that* annoys me."

Danny takes a breath. "Look, I sense you're getting frustrated. I told you we might not find a guy on the first night, but you have to trust—"

"Maybe I don't *want* a guy. Let alone one that *you* find for me."

"Is this because I was critical about your wardrobe earlier?"

"You think this is about clothes? Fucking *clothes??* Look at us!" I gesture at him, then gesture at myself. "Your gorgeous ass is doing me no favors sitting on a stool next to me, pretending to be my hero, when all you are is the hot, sexy flame pulling the moths."

"Look, I'm sorry if I ..." Then he shakes his head and glares at me. "No, I'm not sorry. I tried to help. I thought there was something great between us. We hit it off. We were having fun. I thought—"

"Then why aren't *we* going on a date, huh?"

Danny sputters and scoffs at me. "What?"

"You flirt with me," I accuse him, rising from my stool. Our faces are mere inches apart. "You put your hands in my hair. Telling me my hair is perfect. Complimenting my body. Looking at me at the gym."

"I'm not ..." Either his face is red or the lighting in this place has gone Hellish. "I was just—"

"And so what if I flirt back a little? Who cares? You're not *really* with Joey. He's probably cheating on you. Why aren't you with someone like *me*, Danny? Do *you* even love the guy in the mirror, or was that all a bunch of bullshit?"

"I'm in a relationship," he states, like a declaration. "I'm happy with Joey. I'm not flirting with you. I'm not looking for anyone. I'm—"

"Yeah, I know, you only said it a hundred times already tonight to a hundred different men, none of whom wanted a thing to do with me. And I guess I'm number one hundred and one." I yank my wallet out of my pocket so fast, it fumbles out of my hand. When I go to pick it up off the ground, all its contents fall out. "For fuck's sake," I shout as I start gathering my things off the ground.

A moment passes before I realize Danny has crouched down next to me, helping. We say nothing at all. As we both remain on all fours, picking up my crap from beneath our stools, we remain silent. Then he hands me my cash, my credit card, and a Starbucks gift card I was given for a birthday two years ago and never used. I stuff them away along with some other things that fell out.

He finds something else on the floor. "'The happiest

person is the one who knows themself,'" he reads, then hands it to me. "Fortune cookie?"

I take it and slip it into my wallet. My heart is racing with anger ... or confusion. "It's such a lie. I know myself perfectly, and ... and look at me."

"Are you sure about that?"

I glare at him. "Are *you*?"

He stares back, his full lips parted—his full, plush, velvety lips.

My heart pounds like a drum, staring at them.

Something comes over me.

I lunge forward and press my lips against his.

A split second of terror turns my thumping heart into ice.

Then his lips respond, kissing me back.

Flames. Bombs. Fireworks. Sparkling explosions. Pulse in my ears. The soft touch of his lips. The crackle of electricity in my fingertips.

I grab him by the shirt as our kiss deepens, pulling his face against mine. Then it isn't enough, and my hands slide down his back to take hold of his ass. That only impassions him more as our kiss deepens. After a while, I don't even know where our hands are.

I'm consumed.

Instantly, all of it makes sense. The anger. The confusion. The frustration between us. It's because we both want each other. We can't get enough of each other.

He doesn't want to be my friend. He never did. He's been lying to himself.

I'm the luckiest man in the—

Danny pulls away. "No, no. I can't."

I fall back on my heels, instantly mortified. "Oh, fuck."

"Romeo, I shouldn't have …" Danny shuts his eyes, anguished.

What was I thinking?

"I'm sorry, Danny. This was a terrible idea. I …" He still won't open his eyes. He can't even bear to look at me. I get the message. "I'll go."

I rise from the floor at once, slap enough money on the counter for the both of us, then see myself out of the bar.

9. Games

THE DOG PROUDLY BUYS BOARDWALK.

Everyone groans.

The dice roll again, and the thimble loses some bucks on Baltic Avenue.

The top hat sighs quite wearily and goes to jail, suffering another bout of bad luck.

Then everyone waits for the boot to take its turn.

Everyone continues waiting for that boot.

They wait and they wait.

They wait and—"Oh my god, Rome, seriously, are you even playing??"

I snap out of it and look up.

Prisha stares at me from across the cluttered table full of Monopoly money, hotels, and cards. The 1990s-era box to the game sits askew at the corner of the table, next to one bottle of wine we emptied, and another bottle I'm apparently working my way through.

Juan and Marissa sit on either side of me, tense and on the edges of their seats, awaiting my move.

"I, uh …" I pinch the bridge of my nose, the gesture of which nearly knocks over my wine glass, which I swiftly catch, then decide to down the rest of. Is a migraine coming on? Ugh, it's nearly blinding. "Why is my top hat in jail?"

"You're the boot. The top hat is Marissa," states Prisha rather tersely.

Oh.

Clearly I'm not all here.

"Sorry. I … Wait, wasn't she the wheelbarrow?"

"I didn't like it, and everyone agreed I could be the top hat instead," explains Marissa rather patiently, then shifts her eyes. "Even you."

I don't remember that at all. I reach around to grab the bottle and start refilling my glass. "Do I have enough money to buy a—ugh, my head—a hotel on my, uh—wait, which railroad do I own again?"

"None of them," says Prisha.

"You don't have enough money to buy anything," says Juan.

"Oh." I finish pouring, almost drop the bottle in setting it down, then take a healthy swig before asking: "Can I try—"

"Just roll the damned dice," snaps Prisha.

I pick up the dice with my free hand and toss them at the table.

The dice miss and fall onto the floor.

"Fuck, sorry," I mumble, dizzy, then crouch beneath the table to fetch them.

Prisha has instantly crouched down as well, and now I'm face-to-face with her under the table.

And she's mad. "What in the *hell* is going on with you tonight?" she hisses. "You're a drunken mess!"

"Sorry. I'm totally out of it, I know, my head's not in the game. I have a killer migraine."

"I'm not letting you use that migraine as an excuse. You *gave* yourself that migraine with all of this drinking. I was counting on you tonight, Rome, and—"

"I'm here." I hiccup, blink away a sudden bout of blurriness, then squint at her in the dark. "I'm here. I'll roll the dice."

"You were barely there during charades when I needed you earlier. You practically *threw* that game. How are we supposed to last even a single game of Clue tonight?"

I stare at her in surprise. "We still have a game of Clue to play?"

She sighs with mounting agitation and sits back on her heels. "This is *the only* night we have to play until next week, since my parents are coming, and you're ruining it."

"Not in ..." The room is spinning. "... in ... intentionally, I swear ..."

"Something's up with you, Rome."

I grimace, on all fours beneath the table with Prisha. Honestly, it isn't even about the dice anymore. The darkness down here is exactly what my eyes (and my throbbing head) need. "Maybe I shouldn't be around people tonight," I blurt.

"What?"

"And maybe I also ... can't *stand* my own company." I lower my face to the floor for some reason, resting a cheek on the dirty carpet. "I don't know what I'm feeling. I have a lot on my mind lately. I just ... I just ... I just want to curl up under this table and ... and disappear."

Prisha's brow creases. "Well, you don't have my permission to do that yet."

"I went on another date."

She lifts her head in surprise, and it bumps the table. Rubbing a sore spot and glaring at me, she hisses, "Another date?? When did this happen and why didn't I know?"

"Couple nights ago. It actually wasn't a date. It was ... a date to *get* a date."

"Huh?"

"Danny took me out. He was sort of my wingman or something. We got drinks at a gay bar."

"Danny? Who's Danny?"

Oh, right. "The guy who works at Jimmy's. I mean Jesse's. Whatever it's called."

"Wait," she stops me, lifting a hand. "You mean that cute Asian guy we always see at the front desk every time we go?"

Cute Asian guy ... My heart races with undeserved happiness, hearing those words. Ugh, none of this feels right, not after the way we left things—*not after that fucking kiss I shouldn't have enjoyed.* "Yes, that one. He has a tool of a boyfriend, but he sort of volunteered to help me find a date 'in the real world'. He thinks dating apps are full of lies."

"Well, I agree with him there," mumbles Prisha.

"But it went totally wrong. All the guys were interested in *him*. I was ignored. Blah, blah. Then he and I got into this big fight, and I ..." I slap a hand to my forehead and wipe away sweat that isn't there. I can't mention the kiss. Not yet.

Prisha shakes her head. "That explains why you didn't want to go with us to the gym yesterday or today."

"Yeah. Sorry about that, too." I lie down on my side, sulking. A part of me might be on top of Juan's feet. I can't tell. "I'm pretty much convinced now that I'll be single for-fucking-ever."

"Rome ..."

"All the good guys are taken, and they're all taken by the bad guys. The ass-wipes. The douchebags. The jerks. Is that what it's gonna take?" I ask her, at my wit's end. "Do I have to become a jerk to get a decent guy to even look at me?"

"Um, guys?" mutters Juan, his face appearing suddenly under the table. "We can kinda hear you."

"Yeah," says Marissa, appearing at the other side. "Every word."

"And for the record," says Juan, "I might be straight, but I love you the way you are, Rome. Don't change a thing about yourself. The right guy will come along someday."

"Yeah," agrees Marissa. "I mean, not right now while I'm in jail and Prisha's got Boardwalk and Juan keeps getting nickel-and-dimed at Baltic Avenue. But maybe here in the real world, the right guy is out there for you."

"So how about we roll that dice, huh?" suggests Juan.

I glance at my coworker Juan and Prisha's neighbor Marissa. Their words aren't that encouraging. I still envision my love life as a dark, bottomless abyss full of bitter dissatisfaction and misery. They don't really know me. Maybe not even Prisha.

Maybe not even myself.

Until that fateful night, I wasn't a guy who'd ever dare to kiss someone who has a boyfriend. But there I was, on the sticky floor beneath old bar stools, with my lips locked on the lips of the man of my dreams making the worst mistake of my life.

What is happening to me?

"Yeah," I say anyway. "Let's do it."

I don't win. In fact, I don't think we even finish the game. At some point, I nearly fall out of my chair, then realize I need to sit down somewhere else while the others play. Before I know it, the game is all packed up, Juan and Marissa are gathering their things to leave, and I'm staring at another empty bottle I just finished off, wondering where it all went.

The truth is, Danny was my ideal. He was my ultimate ideal for what I want in a guy.

Maybe there is some sick truth to my fears. I might have thought that one day, he and Joey would break up, and then I'd get my chance. Joey is only in the way—*for now*.

But then I kissed Danny. And now I've selfishly soiled my own dream. I showed him a mountain of insecurities.

My worst shortcomings. My jealousies. My ignorance.

Every worst side of me.

I destroyed the only dream I have left.

"I'm calling you an Uber," says Prisha when it's just us left, Juan and Marissa having gone home.

"Don't," I say, scoffing. "I just live a few blocks away."

She pockets her phone. "Then we're walking." She takes hold of my arm and lifts me out of the chair. "Let's go. *Up!*"

I have no idea how we manage to get out of her apartment, down her stairwell, and onto the street. But here we are, walking side-by-side under the shimmery, pale lights of streetlamps, and she has my arm tucked against her like my life depends on it. Each streetlamp we pass seems screamingly loud and way too bright.

It's at the crosswalk just before my apartment complex that it hits Prisha. "Wait a sec."

Leaning against the light post, I lift a woozy eyebrow her way. "Hmm?"

"Danny. The guy at the gym." She gawks at me. "Is *he* your secret crush you mentioned before?"

I don't know if I have the capacity to even begin this conversation. "I never said that."

"Holy fuck, it totally *is* him. He's your crush? A guy who's already got a boyfriend?"

The crosswalk light turns, but neither of us go. "Okay, I really don't want a lecture. My migraine isn't gone yet, and I'm seeing six of you, and it's hard enough just dealing with *one …*"

"And you went out with him? As your so-called wingman? Are you crazy?"

With each question she bullets at me, I feel dumber and dumber. "Prisha, I know how it sounds …"

"I'm not stupid. You went along with it as an excuse to get closer to your crush." Her eyes turn into two black abysses of condemnation. "He's taken, Rome. He's off-limits. You should have respected his relationship and *not* agreed to go out with him. What were you even thinking?"

I must be a glutton for punishment tonight, because I'm about to say the thing. "That's not the worst of it."

Her harsh eyes flicker. "What do you mean?"

I gaze at the street, unable to meet her eyes when I say it. "I ... kinda accidentally kissed him."

Silence pierces my ears.

Even with the traffic and the noise of the city around us, her silence pierces everything.

"Accidentally ...?"

"Intentionally." I swallow. "I intentionally kissed him. I kissed a taken guy." I clench my fists. "And groped him, too."

"Rome." I feel her disapproval and pity coming off of her in waves. "Rome ..."

The next instant, I'm defensive. "But you haven't met his boyfriend. Really, if you knew the scum Danny is with, you'd know why ... why I ..." I growl with frustration. "He's a fucking *nightmare*, Prisha."

"So what was your endgame here, Rome? Were you planning to convince Danny of that, make him dump his boyfriend, and go out with you instead? By kissing him? And *groping* him? I have a word for that, and it's *not* a gentleman."

"To be fair, I just *was* a gentleman in a top hat in Monopoly, but—"

"You were the boot. Not the top hat. And the boot suits you. Though the dog might've been even more fitting." Her face twists with disappointment. "No matter what his boyfriend is like, that is *Danny's* nightmare to deal with. Not yours. You have a conflict of interest here—especially now that you've gone and made a move on him like a reckless fool—and I don't believe it's right or fair to interfere with their problems."

I lean against the light post again. Traffic roars past us. "Doesn't matter anymore. I ruined what could have been … something."

"Something? You didn't go out that night with an honorable heart, so how can you expect an honorable outcome?"

I hate when she's right. "I have an honorable heart," I say defensively anyway.

"You have a hopeful one, I'll give you that. But you are not being honest with yourself." She shakes her head disapprovingly, then sighs. "I really wish you'd be more responsible with your feelings. Don't let your desperation for a boyfriend make you compromise who you are."

I rub my temples. A wave of anguish keeps piercing my eyeballs. The crosswalk light changes again. The traffic stops. "I'm basically home already. You can go back to your place now. I think I can make it across a street without dying."

"Don't compromise who you are," she repeats as I start to cross the street. "I mean it, Rome. Don't compromise who you are for *anyone*."

Her words linger and haunt me long after I reach my building and start ascending the stairs, my head throbbing and spinning. I know Prisha is walking back to her place filled with pity for me. Or disapproval. Or a more polite version of disgust, whatever that is.

I promise you, Prisha, whatever disappointment you feel can't possibly match the disappointment I feel in myself.

My cold, dark apartment stays cold and dark as I lie on the couch, the room spinning around me.

It's an especially cruel irony, to be so infatuated with someone who's not only taken, but now likely can't stand your very existence.

All because of a stupid kiss.

Danny made a great point before we left for our night out, didn't he? *'Fall in love with the guy in the mirror first before you dare to give your heart to anyone else.'*

Is that where I've been wrong this whole time?

Suddenly I'm in the bathroom staring at myself in the mirror. My greasy face. My messy hair. Some unexplained red spot on my cheek, maybe from when I laid it down on that dirty carpet, probably picking up some face disease.

Do I love that guy in the mirror? This sweet, hopeful, patient guy who has so much love to give, but no one in the whole fucking world to give it to?

This Mr. Nice Guy …?

What has "being nice" gotten me, anyway? Other than walked all over, misunderstood, and taken advantage of? Is this really what I am?

10. The Dog

THERE'S THIS RINGING IN MY EARS, EXCEPT I THINK I MIGHT be imagining it.

I'm almost certain I'm imagining it.

It's a day just like any other day. Friday, in fact. I go to work. I meet with Prisha and the others on my team, and no one mentions game night. We are updated on our tasks by our supervisor Mr. Milton—who didn't seem impressed with our last assignment, standing over our shoulders and muttering, "Hm," every few minutes as he looks over our work. After he gives us a butt load of new tasks, we busy ourselves among a circle of desks crowded by laptops, notebooks, and half-empty coffee cups, wondering why we put up with him.

And all day in the back of my head, Prisha's words from last night keep haunting me. *'Don't compromise who you are for anyone.'* I can't help but wonder what they really mean.

Who am I, exactly?

What have I been compromising?

When five o'clock hits, we gather our things, take the elevator trip down to the first floor, and approach the doors to

Jesse's Fitness. It's the first time I've been here since the "incident". Prisha is so busy chatting with Juan and the two other coworkers joining us that she doesn't take note of the dead look on my face. They laugh at a joke as they push through the doors, me trailing behind, then make their way for the treadmills.

As my friends start up their playlists and machines, I just stand at the foot of mine and gaze out at the rest of the gym, lost in thought. The echoing clanging and banging of metal against metal fill my ears, but it still doesn't kill the imaginary ringing in them. That ringing is stronger than everything today. Stronger than the muscled guys in tight shirts getting sweaty. Stronger than their thick legs and puffed up chests. Stronger than the noise of their grunting, growling, and obnoxious slamming of weights to the floor.

Stronger than the ghost of Danny's kiss, which still lives on my lips.

I really shouldn't have done that.

I spot a guy around my age sitting at one of the weight machines—the bicep curl machine. He looks like me, except half my weight, twice as dorky, and positively terrified. He shakes nervously as he attempts to do a few reps on one of the lowest weight settings. He wears an over-sized athletic shirt, his bony arms barely touching the sleeves. His gym shorts are loose and baggy. As he does his curls, his entire body trembles from the effort.

Some puffy muscle dude comes right up to him. "You done yet?" he grunts. The skinny guy looks up, smiles politely, then quickly vacates the machine. I watch him as he stands off to the side while the puffy bodybuilder goes to town pushing weights and letting them slam down with every rep.

And the skinny guy just stares at him.

And I watch it all.

I can see everything written across that sad dude's face: his own fantasy of becoming big and muscled someday, his hopes and dreams, his undying determination. He probably thinks he'll finally be noticed if he can get his arms bigger. Just add a little more muscle to his body, and he will no longer be invisible to the world.

That's his life's plan. His goal. His everything. And he's going to do it no matter what.

And it breaks my heart, watching that guy, reading his sad, hopeful face, while my ears continue to ring, ring, ring.

That faint, faraway, restless ringing ... so tiny, so empty, almost not even there.

Yet it's stronger than all of the muscle and noise in this room.

And I still don't know what it is.

Probably just a hangover.

Is that guy me? Am I that pathetic loser standing next to the bicep curl machine, too nice to assert myself to some muscled-up dude, too desperate for attention to care about how sad I look?

"Rome ...?"

I snap out of it. It's Prisha, bringing me back to the real world. "Right, sorry." I get on the treadmill, press the button, then start walking. I stare ahead and mind nothing except my feet and where I place them next. I don't put on my usual playlist. I doubt I can concentrate on anything anyway.

Not with the—

Slam! That bicep machine keeps clanging loudly with every rep the muscled guy does. *Slam!* Each time it crashes, I swear I feel the building shake. *Slam!* I don't even have to look; I know the skinny dude is still standing there like a useless twig, waiting for his turn again. *Slam!*

It's making the ringing in my ears louder.

Slam!

And louder.

Slam!

Until quite suddenly I have to do something about it. I shut off my treadmill and step off. The gym is a jungle of metal and leather and sweat as I cut through the aisles of machines. I worm my way through, dodging each one, stepping over lost dumbbells and weights that try to catch my feet like vines on the forest floor.

Soon, I'm standing in front of the muscled dude at the bicep machine. *Right* in front of him. So close, he could curl me instead if he wanted.

"Excuse me."

The dude only now looks up, as if my proximity wasn't enough to catch his attention. His face wrinkles as he looks me over. "Huh?"

"My friend here was using this machine."

The skinny guy, who I'm standing next to, and who most certainly is not my friend, stares at me in bewilderment as I confront this puffed-up asshole. Said asshole is staring at me, too. It's as if I just broke some unspoken rule, to ever dare interrupt a jackhole like this in the middle of his set.

I don't know what's come over me, but that ringing in my ears won't stop.

All I'm seeing is red.

"Did you hear me?" I snap, my voice cracking like a whip. "I said my friend was using this machine before you shoved him off of it."

"Huh? I didn't shove him off of it. I asked if he was done."

"And he was too polite to say he *wasn't* done. Did he look *done* to you?" I point at the guy. "He was in the middle of a bicep curl when you asked. I saw it."

The guy's face is contorted with a mixture of amusement and indignation as he gives my scrawny new pretend-friend half a glance. "He could barely push ten pounds. He was *playing* with the machine. I actually want to use it."

"I don't care how much he does, nor how much *you* do. You don't own this gym. We have just as much a right to be here as you do."

"Fine, he can finish his so-called 'set' then, no need to cry and bitch about it." He rises from the machine, giving each of us a look. "This isn't a playground. Some of us take this seriously, you know." He slowly struts away. "Fucking whacko," he mutters over a shoulder.

I have barely a second to recover from the anger still bubbling in my chest when the skinny guy steps in front of me. "You really didn't have to do that."

"Yeah, I did."

"You really didn't. But it was cool. But also terrifying. But mostly cool. My name's Jonty, by the way."

I turn to him. "Jonty? I've never met a Jonty."

"It's short for Jonathan, actually."

"I'm Rome. Short for Romeo."

"Oh." He thinks it over. "I've never met a Romeo. Except for the Shakespeare one. I mean, I didn't *meet* him, obviously, he's fictional. I just meant—"

I cut to the chase. "You have to stand up for yourself, Jonathan. You can't let assholes like that walk all over you. You were at this machine first. You were in the middle of doing curls."

"It's fine, really. He was—*oh, you called me by my full name, just noticed*—That guy belongs here, okay? He's here all the time. Maybe he's preparing for a bodybuilding competition or something. I don't really know what I'm doing anyway," he jokes, chuckling.

His joking and chuckling only makes me angrier. "Of course you know what you're doing. You know how this machine works. You're not an idiot, are you?"

He blinks. "N-No."

"No, you're not. You *let* him shove you off of this machine, shoving you out of your own kingdom. While you're on that machine, *you're* king of the castle, Jonathan. Fuck that guy. Don't let that happen ever again. No one has power over you except yourself."

"I … Well, I mean … He didn't *shove* me, per se. He didn't even touch me, actually."

I narrow my eyes at him. "Jonathan, our friendship isn't

off to a great start."

He blinks. "Friendship …?"

Just then, I catch sight of someone quickly approaching me in my peripheral. I barely have time to turn before the body slams against mine, then pins me to the wall. The movement is so sudden, it takes me a second to realize what's even happened.

Then I look into the face of my assailant.

Oh. It's Joey.

Fucking perfect.

"I'm gonna say this once," he growls in my face, low and threatening. "Stay away from Danny."

I notice the muscled dude I just scared off the bicep machine is behind him, watching this unfold.

Great. I guess they're friends. I poked the bear's buddy, and the bear realized who I was, and now I'm pristinely fucked.

"You hear me?" Joey grunts, his body somehow pressing even more firmly against mine. I don't know if that's a belt buckle, a phone, or a hard dick I'm feeling against my thigh, but it's there, and it's suddenly all I can focus on. "If you ever make a move on my boyfriend again, I'm gonna do a lot more than just shove you against this wall."

I stare into his raging, charcoal eyes. My face tightens.

I just realized I'm missing a key ingredient that any normal person would have in this situation: *fear.*

"Sorry, Joey," I say, "but I'm confused. Are you trying to threaten me … or turn me on?"

Joey's eyes flash indignantly.

His buddy behind him gawps at me.

My new friend Jonty doesn't know what to make of any of this, his face as expressionless as a towel.

Joey steps back from me, eyes darkened with disdain. "You heard me loud and clear," he says, apparently deciding to ignore my taunt. "Stay away from my boyfriend or else your ass is mine."

"Again, still can't tell."

"You've been warned," he growls, shaking his head, then he storms off. His buddy lingers for a second, and I swear I see the tiniest hint of amusement on his face before he follows Joey, the two of them heading to the locker room.

And as I watch them go, my own anger fades, traded instantly for guilt. After all, I *did* kiss Joey's boyfriend. Intentionally. With ulterior motives. And none of that makes me proud.

Joey has every right to be mad at me.

But does he even know I kissed his boyfriend? Or does he only know I went out with Danny? What exactly did Danny tell him?

Jonty appears in front of me suddenly. "Now *that*, I would classify as a shove."

I squint at him. "What?"

"And you were *amazing*." He shakes his head in wonder. "I mean, what was that even about? They were gonna kick your ass, and you stood up to them like some kind of … of superhero *badass*! Who is this Danny guy, anyway? Is Danny that guy's boyfriend? Oh! Did you try to steal Danny from him or something??"

This new friend of mine is rather easily excitable. Like a little puppy. "Kinda."

"Hmm. You shouldn't have done that. I mean, I've had crushes on girls who had boyfriends, but I'd never act on it. It isn't right." He frowns at himself. "Not that they'd be into me, anyway."

And my new puppy friend is straight. Interesting.

I face him. "Listen, Jonathan. You saw how that Joey guy was, right? A total asshole? And his buddy is the dickhead who took over your machine."

Jonty shrugs. "So?"

"Those guys—assholes, dickheads, *jerks*—they think they run the world. All of them. And you know what?" I get in Jonty's face. "They do."

"They do?"

"Fuck yeah, they do. Is there a jerk in your life? Like … a really, *really* big jerk? Someone who gives you hell? Someone who makes you angry? Someone who makes your life goddamned miserable?"

The words seem to shake him. His gaze drops to the floor, his eyes like two tiny stones. "My big brother. He definitely hit every branch on his way down the asshole tree, for sure. He does whatever he wants. He gets away with it all. My parents don't say it, but he's their favorite." Jonty sighs. "I hate it."

I throw an arm around his back, then make him face the rest of the gym. "Every jerk in the world is your asshole big bro. They're your crush's boyfriend. They're your boss who makes ten times more than you ever will. They're all of these guys at the gym who look down on you as if their protein-fattened bodies give them some magic authority over your own happiness."

"You're right."

I turn him to face me, then grab my new friend by his bony shoulders. "You don't get the girl of your dreams by being nice. You get the girl by being *them*. Otherwise, they will always take the girl you want ... and the guy I want."

"Is your guy Danny ...?"

My heart squeezes with anguish at the sound of his name, like the name is a literal fist slamming into my chest, a set of vengeful knuckles straight to the heart.

I take a breath, then nod.

"I see," he murmurs thoughtfully.

"I don't know about you, Jonathan, but I don't intend to die being a Mr. Nice Guy. What has *smiling* all the time gotten us? What has *nice* ever gotten us? It's time for us to take control. It's time for us to learn from our enemies. From these jerks." My eyes harden. "No more nice, Jonathan."

"I go by Jonty."

"Not anymore. Jonty's the twig who lets guys take over his machine. Jonty's the little brother who'll always get overlooked by Mommy and Daddy. Jonty's the nice guy." My eyes darken. "You're Jonathan from now on. Own it."

"Hmm. Well, then you've gotta be Romeo," he decides, lifting his chin to me. Then his eyes flash worriedly and he recoils. "Uh, sorry. I mean, only if you *want* to be Romeo."

"Sorry?" I snort. "Did you just say 'sorry' to me ...? Jonathan doesn't apologize."

"He doesn't?"

"Nope. *Jonty* used to. But *Jonathan* apologizes to no one and for nothing."

A flame lights up in his eyes. He nods. "Romeo doesn't apologize either, does he?"

I mull it over. Suddenly, it sounds right. I give him a smirk of approval. "Romeo doesn't."

"Hmm. Jonathan ..." He nods. "Yeah. I like it. Jonathan." His eyes meet mine, self-assured and ready. "No more nice."

A thought suddenly occurs to me. When I glance over my shoulder, I notice my coworkers have finished their session. They're gathered by the treadmills chatting amongst each other and laughing.

But Prisha stands apart from them, unengaged, watching me from across the gym. Maybe she's been watching this whole scene unfold. On her face, there's an expression of profound mystification, as if she can't for the life of her make sense of anything she's seeing. Like she's a stranger, peering through someone else's window, confounded and lost.

Like she doesn't know who I am anymore. Doesn't recognize me. Doesn't know her best friend.

It's a look I'm certain I'll remember for ages.

And it's while I stare at her that I realize the ringing in my ears is gone. A sense of calmness and certainty I have never known before has taken me over like a magic spell. I feel capable of anything suddenly. I feel freed. I feel energized. I know exactly what I have to do.

"No more nice," I recite back, still gazing across the gym at a life I'm now certain I have to leave behind.

One Year Later

11. Bad Guys

I SLAM HIS BACK AGAINST THE KITCHEN WALL.

A plastic bowl and a spoon topple from the counter nearby and crash to the floor.

His eyes flash with surprise as my lips descend onto his neck, then devour their way south. His shirt is in the way, so I rip it open. He gasps with surprise. I hope this wasn't his favorite shirt. Also, I don't care. I press a row of kisses across his chest to his nipple, where I cause it to harden beneath the flat of my tongue. Then I trade it for a sadistic nip with my teeth, and he responds by filling my kitchen with a groan of delirious pleasure.

They always groan with delirious pleasure.

Fast-forward however long, and I've got the guy naked and bent over the arm of my couch. Isn't that how it always happens? To be more accurate, he isn't fully naked; his socks are still on, which he didn't have time to pull off before I took him over like a ragdoll.

The condom is on, I'm lubed up, and I'm fucking him with my eyes closed. My hands grip his waist so firmly, he doesn't go anywhere. He's tight, and my raging-hard cock is feeling every slick, electric thrust as I pound him deeply. The fleshy claps I make against his ass as our bodies ram together fill my ears like the drum line to my favorite song, further textured by the rhythmic creaking of my couch as it protests. The music is ruined only by his annoying grunts, which come in a perfect rhythm as I fuck him—and escalate in pitch the longer we go.

The truth is, he could be any guy in the world.

This could be any ass. Any groan. Anyone. It doesn't matter. It's doing its intended purpose tonight: getting me off.

Except for that annoying grunt he keeps making.

Finally, I've had enough. I pull out, flip him over, and toss him at the couch onto his back. He gasps, wide-eyed, as I come forward, throw his legs over my shoulders, and start fucking him from the front. His jaw drops to his chest as I pump him hard and rough, staring into his face and gripping him. "Oh my *god!* Oh my *god!*" he cries out, his voice trembling with delight. I guess he's traded his annoying grunting for praying to the Holy Father. And it isn't even Sunday. "Oh my *god!* Oh my *god!* Oh my *g*—"

My hand slaps over his mouth, muffling him.

I shut my eyes and keep fucking him like a manic animal. He slobbers against my palm as he continues to moan unintelligibly. I'm getting close, racing toward the edge, hungry for release.

The edge passes me by faster than expected.

I come so hard, I can't feel anything but floating, weightless, merry bliss.

Every single time, it seems to last forever, this euphoric reward.

And then it ends so quickly.

Fast-forward ten minutes later, I'm standing on my balcony in just my underwear with a glass of sparkling rosé at my lips. It's no longer my sad drink; it's my celebratory drink, and I have it every time after a good night's fuck. A glass of rosé is basically my post-lay cigarette.

"Can I ask a question?"

I don't even turn around. "Nope."

"Who were you thinking about when you fucked me?"

I take a sip of my drink. I have no idea what the dude's getting at, but the fact that he hasn't left yet is getting annoying. I glance over my shoulder. "You're still not dressed."

He sighs as he slips on his shirt, then inspects a stain as he talks. "It's obvious you go somewhere mentally. Your eyes are always closed."

They always get feely and talky afterwards. "So?"

"I was just wondering. I'm not hurt or anything. Actually, you can totally tell me who it is. Is it an ex of yours?"

"Why aren't you gone yet?"

"Can't find my phone. Also, you tore my shirt. That was really hot at the time, but … this was my favorite one."

"You'll find a new favorite."

"This is a designer brand, too. *Ugh, where'd I put my phone …?* Really, it's okay to tell me who you were thinking about. You know … for next time."

Next time, he says. Adorable. "I don't do next times."

"Maybe we could role-play, if you wanted." He obviously ignored my remark. "I could be him, if that's what gets you going."

I freeze, my glass not quite to my lips.

No one can ever be the man I think about. No one will ever be him. No one can ever compare.

"Or," I say, "you could be the guy who just left my apartment and stopped *lingering* like some sad fucking puppy who won't shut up."

Silence. I glance over my shoulder to find him at the end of the couch, phone in hand.

"Found it," he says, deflated.

Staring at his face, something clicks inside of me. Maybe it's the last shred of compassion I still have left in me, rattling around inside my heart like spare change. "Sorry." I face the balcony again. "I'm ... not really myself lately."

He doesn't respond for a moment. Then I hear his feet shuffle as he moves to the door. It opens. He stops again. "Whoever broke your heart," he says, "must've been one outstanding guy. I hope you find someone like that again."

The door closes behind him.

And just like that, my peace returns. I down the rest of my glass, and another night comes to an end.

One outstanding guy, he said.

I smirk and shake my head.

The next time I open my eyes, it's morning, and long stripes of sunlight are the only companions in my bed.

I throw a comb through my hair. The man in the mirror stares back at me. He looks like someone I used to know, but can't quite place his name. He lets his stubble grow out now, rugged and reckless. His face is more chiseled and brawny than I remember, too. That's probably due to his annoyingly persistent and aggressive workout and diet regimen, which shows all over his toned body. His shoulders are bigger and more broad. His stomach is flatter, too. His arms are always pumped.

His eyes are sharp with confidence.

He takes shit from no one.

I admire that guy in the mirror.

Today when I stroll through the doors of Bold Brands Marketing Firm, I go straight to the coffee. For some reason, Juan moves out of the way as I pour myself a cup. After a second of hesitation, he asks how I'm doing. I answer with a grunt. He says something else about the weather and makes a joke, but I ignore it as I stir my cup with a tiny stick.

Until he says, "She's back."

My stirring stops. I know exactly who he's talking about. Still, I ask: "Who?"

"She was reassigned to our team again. To, uh … help with the new fitness campaign, I guess." He shuffles his feet. "I just thought you'd like to know. Heads-up or whatever." He cradles his cup and departs the room, leaving me be.

She's back.

I resume stirring my cup, but contemplatively now.

When I head to our main workroom, I spot her at the round table right away. She looks the same. Not a single change to even be mentioned. The others are greeting her and welcoming her back after her number of months working at the sister building, teasing her about being gone for so long. There's only one empty seat available at the table—the one right next to her. As I approach, an unmistakable tension fills the air, slowly suffocating the joyous chatter until all that's left is an eerie, uncertain silence. I take my seat, then slurp a sip of coffee, paying the silence no mind.

"Hello, Rome," she greets me stiffly.

"Prisha," I greet her back, then set my cup on the table in front of me.

Eyes shift around the room, unsure what to say.

Everyone knows the situation. It's no secret how our friendship crumbled a year ago after I made a new best friend at the gym. I don't want to blame Prisha completely, but she kept nagging me, criticizing my life choices, judging me when I started lifting instead of just dwelling on the treadmills, then threw a tantrum when I stopped going to Jesse's altogether after finding a better gym elsewhere. Then she stopped inviting me over for game nights, we got into a fight over nothing, she was relocated to another building across town for the past few months, and that was that.

Now she's back.

I hate having to act civil.

And over my morning coffee, too.

Mr. Milton cuts all of the ice when he saunters into the room rather abruptly and tosses a stack of folders into the center of the round table. "Hm. I don't know why I even bother," he drawls, eyelids half open, a mug in his other hand, "but the campaign the other team developed doesn't cut it. The copy is boring and uninspired. The photos they used are sophomoric and done-before. There are so many damned holes in their notes, I could strain pasta through it." He sighs and leans against the table. "You guys need to put your big brains together and do better than this garbage. A fitness business is paying Bold Brands big bucks to broaden their clientele, they're giving us one more chance, and we still haven't delivered. I want edgy. I want strong. I want smart. Amateur hour is *over*."

At once, everyone in the room starts engaging, throwing their ideas onto the table, discussing, and brainstorming. But nothing they say even remotely inspires a look of approval from Mr. Milton, who just listens on with the same bored expression, like the man is running on an hour's sleep.

Then his eyes find mine. "And what are you planning to contribute today, Romeo, other than that sourpuss attitude on your face?"

I lift my face to him and quirk an eyebrow.

The room draws silent at once.

Mr. Milton squints at me. "The difference between me and you is that I'm paid to have attitude. You're paid to give me good ideas. And so far, you're contributing nothing."

I nod. "Alright. I'll give you an idea." I sit forward. "Hit up a gym now and then to blow off steam. Maybe try this fitness company that hired us to do their busywork. Tons of little men like you enjoy going to the gym and feeling big and powerful. That way, you don't have to take it out on us that all you are is a weak, bitter fellow who's overly pent-up because his wife's not putting out."

His eyes flash indignantly. "Excuse me?"

"I think you heard me. You are one pent-up little tyrannosaurus today." I shrug as I take hold of my coffee. "Hey, look, I'm just stating facts. Don't come at me just 'cause you're not getting any."

Silence pierces the air.

Mr. Milton stares at me from across the table.

Frigid, icy, uninterrupted silence.

Until Juan snaps his fingers. "Holy crap, that's it!" Everyone turns to him. "What Romeo just said! 'Don't come at me just 'cause you're not getting any.' That's perfect for the direction of the campaign!"

At first, no one follows.

Then someone else jumps in. "Oh. You mean ... selling the idea that you gotta go to the gym, get buff and sexy, in order to ... get some?"

"Yeah!" says Juan. "Like, if you wanna get some, pump some."

"Get some of this to get some of that," throws in someone else, starting up a brainstorm.

"Come at me all you want, but at least I'm getting some," says another guy, to a few chuckles.

As the ideas roll in, the look on Mr. Milton's face slowly changes. It's like he forgot I said anything at all. His eyes are open as he listens, seeing the bigger picture. He turns his head to each person, taking in every new idea. In truth, it's uncertain what he's making of all of this.

But someone decides to make it very clear what *they* think: "This is totally juvenile."

Everyone turns her way.

It's Prisha.

"I mean, seriously?" She glances at everyone else at the table. "Romeo just insulted Mr. Milton. He wasn't proposing some brilliant new advertising idea. 'Get some'? Selling the idea of this gym based on how much sex it'll get you? That's so ... obscene."

Juan leans in to the guy next to him. "*She's* obviously not gettin' any." Everyone hears despite his lowered voice, and the room fills with laughter.

Prisha folds her arms and sits back, unfazed by the mockery. "I don't like it. I think it's lazy, I think it's juvenile, and I think it promotes a ... rather *depraved* and primitive point of view. There is more to life than sex. Why don't we take the opposite angle? 'Beauty is more than superficial.' Or perhaps something health-related? It's popular nowadays to be fit and healthy. I'm even keen on leaning into frequenting the gym as a *trendy fad* to do with your girlfriends or guy friends. But I do *not* think our best foot forward is to sell a gym membership with *sex*."

The silence in the room is the only reply she gets.

Piercing, defiant silence.

Until Mr. Milton clears his throat. "Everything today is sold with sex. I like this 'getting some' angle. Run with it." Then he shoots me a look. "Good thinking, Romeo. Even if it was at my expense." He snorts, cracks a smile, then takes his mug and himself out of the room to let us work.

As everyone begins to explode with new ideas, Prisha stares at the side of my face, dumbfounded.

I just sip my coffee and kick back.

With an inspired room full of talking, chatter, and clacking keyboards, the day comes to a fast end. I get on the elevator while texting my buddy Jonathan that I'm on the way to the gym.

Prisha slips into the elevator the moment before the doors shut, causing them to open again.

We stand side-by-side in silence as the elevator doors decide whether they're ready to close. It's unclear if Prisha knew I was already on the elevator or this is a totally unintended situation she just put herself in.

Finally the doors decide to close, then we descend.

The two of us continue standing in silence.

I feel her glance at me. For some reason, I can tell it isn't a look of hatred. It feels soft somehow. Thoughtful. Almost like she's trying to see the old me buried deep down somewhere in the stranger she's sharing an elevator with.

It's going to take her a while.

When we reach the first floor, I hesitate a moment before stepping out. Prisha walks by my side until she stops at the entrance to Jesse's Fitness, but doesn't yet go inside, as I walk on. It's when I'm just about to leave the building that I hear her call to my back, "Take care of yourself, Rome."

I stop at the doors. For some reason, I can't face her. "You too," I say without looking, then leave.

The walk to my new gym isn't very far, but it feels like it's on the other side of the world suddenly. Maybe that's because all of my thoughts are on Prisha's sudden reappearance in my life and the way she regarded me. Really, she should be proud of me now. No one's talked back to Mr.

Milton that way and survived. Hell, he even seemed to like it. Not to mention that my attitude was the catalyst that got everyone's brain juices flowing. Prisha and I used to talk about how someone should set him straight someday. Didn't I just do that?

I guess nothing I do will ever be good enough for her.

Just one glance of her all-knowing eyes, and I feel like I'm supposed to be ashamed of something. Isn't shame the exact emotion I've been trying to rid myself of over this past year? Screw that. I won't let her make me feel ashamed. I'm better, stronger, and more confident than I've ever been in my life.

For someone who knows everything, she sure seems to know nothing.

It's a good thing we're not friends anymore.

I push through the doors of Weights & Mates with such aggression, it causes the walls to shake. I go straight to the locker room to change, claiming a locker right next to my buddy, who's already half-changed and tying his shoes. I'm so ready to sweat my ass off tonight for the cause. I start fishing around inside my backpack for my workout clothes.

"Uh, are you even gonna say hi to me?"

I glance down at Jonathan on the bench. "Hi." Then I continue fishing.

"Damn. You're in a mood."

"Weird day at work. Just try not to walk in the crossfire, I can't help it today." I find my shorts and tank finally, yank them free, then start changing.

"I've got some details added to my tat yesterday. Wanna

see?" He watches me change for a moment, forgetting his shoes. Then he frowns. "Hey, what's going on with you?"

I pull off my shirt and pitch it into my locker like I'm angry at it. "Weird day at work, I already said."

"You've barely looked at me."

I sigh and turn to my friend.

What was once my emaciated twin comprised of nothing but skin and bone, is now a firm-bodied man with a toned yet slender swimmer's build. Though his eyes still appear permanently shrunken in terror, he sure doesn't look like a twig anyone can snap in half anymore. He's sporting black gym shorts and a loose Nirvana t-shirt with the sleeves torn off—which is how I instantly spot all of the details that have been added to his half-sleeve tattoo that covers his left bicep. It definitely had an unfinished vibe before. Now it looks like a full, vibrant scene of tension between a demon and an angel, encircled by thorny vines and fire.

I lift my eyebrows. "Nice."

"Yeah, it's pretty sick, huh?" He gives his arm an inspection. "Still gotta add some more color to the flames. Not quite satisfied yet, but I like the artist's work. Last time my big brother saw this, he looked terrified of me. Mission accomplished." His eyes meet mine. "Really, you can tell me what's going on. Maybe I have advice."

His advice is a sad, inadequate replacement for Prisha's. Anything Jonathan suggests for me to do begins and ends with some form of our mantra we developed the day we met: just do what you feel like and apologize for nothing. Needless to say, it doesn't apply well to every situation in life.

"I already have the perfect advice for myself," I tell him, shutting my locker. "Work out until nothing's on my mind but my dick and whoever I'm gonna stick it in tonight."

Jonathan—who is the literal dictionary opposite of a prude—grins with approval. "Hell yeah!"

The pair of us head out to the main gym. We go straight for the free weights and claim a pair of benches, where we start our usual sets with the dumbbells. When we move to the bench press, I spot him, encouraging him like a trainer. He does the same for me. We're like an oddly perfect team of losers who got sick of losing and did something about it. Now we're winners. A full year of commitment and dedication later, we're part of the crowd that used to shove us out.

Now, no one shoves us out.

"Ready to get out of here?" he grunts after we finish a round of squats. We're drenched in sweat.

"Yeah. Hitting up King's tonight?"

"Always has the best mix of hot babes for me and loose guys for you," Jonathan reasons. "Whatever new club we tried last weekend sucked. Shouldn't mess with the tried and true, know what I mean?" He gets his things and makes his way to the locker room. After a second, I grab my own towel, fling it over my shoulder, then turn to head there myself.

I stop at once, nearly crashing into someone I didn't see right behind me.

"Watch it!" I shout by reflex.

Then my eyes zero in on the face of the guy I almost walked into.

His beautiful face—*Danny*.

12. You're Sweaty

MY HEART RACES UP TO MY THROAT.

In the space of a second, I have become my small, passionate, weak-in-the-knees former self.

He meets my stunned gaze with surprise. Then a look of absolute joy washes over his face as he recognize me. "Romeo?"

I can barely speak. "D-Danny?"

Our faces are mere inches apart, since we'd come so close to crashing into each other. Neither of us back away, as if just our eyes hold us in place.

"I haven't seen you in …" Danny lets out half a laugh. "I don't even know how long."

I can't help myself. "What're you doing at this gym?"

"Oh. I, um …" His lips are still as kissable as ever. His eyes are tender and sweet. He's wearing just gym shorts and a tight, ribbed, white tank top, his honey-brown skin gleaming with sweat. His hair is a quirky, adorable mess with a cowlick in the front *and* the back. "I should start with saying I don't work at Jesse's anymore."

"Really? Why?"

"Oh, a few reasons. Change of management. And everything is still super outdated and rundown over there. I actually got a new job at this really cool vitamin and nutritional supplements store and am doing *much* better. My boss Denise is amazing. Lots of gay clientele and coworkers. I'm paid more, too. Been trying out new gyms in the area and just heard about this place. It's close to my apartment."

"That sounds great."

"Thanks!"

Neither of us have backed away.

The sexual tension is rampant and unrelenting.

"It's … *really* nice to see you again, Romeo."

I almost can't stand the effect he has over me, even after all this time. "You, too."

He takes one measly step back, yet still feels close enough to taste. His eyes drop to my chest as he takes in the rest of me. "Wow, you look great. You've clearly worked out a lot since I last saw you."

"Yeah. I have."

My thoughts are jumbled. My confidence is gone. *What is happening to me?*

Something dark and fiery swells in my chest, sensing my panic, and it takes over. It's a beast within me that I've trained over the past year—a beast I rely on, a beast that has protected my heart, a beast that knows what to do in a vulnerable situation like this.

My face hardens. A smirk curls my lips. I let out a grunt. "What? Didn't think I had it in me to get buff?"

Danny looks up at me, surprised. "Huh? Oh, no. I mean, yes. I mean, no. I ..." He laughs and blushes, then takes another step back. "I'm just surprised a little, that's all."

"Surprised? Sounds like you didn't have any faith in me." I cross my arms and lean against a nearby machine, ignoring all the anxiety and excitement racing around my system. I adopt my impenetrable steel armor that is the beast. My face is a rock-hard mask of emotional immunity. "Well, drink it all in. I'm a new person now. Hmm, and I see *you're* still a cute little snack."

His eyes flash. "You think I'm a—?" He lets out another laugh. "Snack. Okay, I guess I can go with that. Thanks ... or something?" He clears his throat and shakes his head. "You really *have* changed a lot since the last time we saw each other."

"If I remember right, the last time we saw each other, we made out on the floor of a gay bar. Then I felt shitty and ran away like a scared little boy." My eyes lock onto his. "I can assure you, if it was the *new me* who kissed you that night, I sure wouldn't run away." *What am I saying? Stop talking.* "I'd take you back to my place. I'd keep kissing you all over until you couldn't remember your own name. It'd be more than just your pretty mouth I'd be kissing, too." *Oh my god, stop, stop, stop.* "You think you're surprised with me now? You have no idea the beast I've become since we last spoke."

The humor flees from his eyes and is replaced with genuine surprise.

For one terrifying second, I know I've lost him.

The new Romeo is too much. He's gone too far.

110

Then the tiniest smile plays upon his lips. "Apparently I don't know the beast you've become. But I think I like him."

His lips disarm me immediately.

They drain the confidence from my veins. Shrinking me. Paralyzing me.

The feelings haven't gone away; they've grown tenfold.

Danny shrugs. "Anyway, I should probably let you get to the locker room. You look ..." His eyes stray to my chest once again. "... sweaty."

"Yeah, well ..." I'm struggling to keep this act up. "From the look of your eyes, seems like you're all about this man funk. Almost like you can't get enough of it."

What in the actual fuck am I saying?

Danny bites his lip, then meets my eyes.

I stare back, astonished.

Is it working? Is this actually working? Is he into this new-me?

"Guess I'll see you around," I tell him. "Enjoy subtly checking out my ass as I head off." Then I push away from the machine and make my way to the locker room. And of course I give a look over my shoulder, and there Danny is, watching me as I go.

But his eyes aren't on my ass; they're on my face.

He looks hopeful. Happy. Curious.

Then he says, "Hey, Romeo?"

I stop at the door. "Yeah?"

"Do you want to ... get a drink sometime?"

Oh my god.

Like a cloud eclipsing the sun, something heavy hits me.

I frown at him. "And what about Joey?"

For a second, he appears confused. Then he chuckles and shakes his head. "Oh, that's not a problem anymore. There … There isn't any more Joey." His mouth twists awkwardly. "We split up a while ago."

They split up.

They split up.

"Oh," is all I can say, stunned.

"Maybe this weekend or something? Friday at seven?" he offers.

The invisible emotion-hiding mask pops right back over my face, but I'm pretty sure it's sitting askew. "Uh, yeah, sure. Doesn't make a difference to me."

"Meet outside your place again?"

"Whatever floats your goat." *Goat??* "Boat. Your, uh … boat."

Danny is still too sweet to laugh at me. He just smiles. "See you then."

I'm a statue of strength and self-control. I give him a nod, turn, and march my way to the locker room door, parting ways with the man of my dreams as if he's nothing but a business associate.

Then I finally get inside the locker room.

And at once, the mask falls straight off and shatters on the floor. I slam shut the door and press my back against it, instantly converted into my panicked, shrunken, confused self from a year ago.

Out of breath. Eyes wide. Mouth agape.

Emotionally frantic.

Joey is out of the picture.

Danny is single.

And he just asked me out.

What the fuck is happening to my life today?

Jonathan appears in front of me, already changed out of his sweaty workout clothes. "Hey, man. What's going on? Got yourself a hot piece of ass already?" He lifts an eyebrow. "Whoa, dude, you look freaked out."

And Danny is just as kissable as ever. Cute. Sexy. Boyish laugh and muscle-man bod. Cuddly and sweet. Polite and self-aware and intelligent. Sensitive. Everything I've ever wanted in a guy. He hasn't changed one bit.

Except for the giant fucking fact that he ditched the douchebag he used to call a boyfriend.

Now nothing's in the way.

Except myself.

13. Tough

So ... REMEMBER THAT WHOLE "JONATHAN IS TERRIBLE AT advice" thing?

"Let me get this straight." Jonathan sits on my kitchen counter, frowning at a cabinet door across from him as he squints in thought. We came straight to my place after the gym to figure this out. "Your Danny guy you're obsessed with is back in your life, he goes to our gym, and he's single now?"

"Yep, yep, and yep." I take a sip of my protein shake, leaning against the opposite counter.

"And you're gonna go have a drink with him Friday night?"

"Yep."

Jonathan shrugs. "I don't see what you're so freaked out about. This is great, isn't it? Now you can finally score the guy of your dreams. Bang him good. Bend him over literally any piece of furniture you've got in this place."

"It's not like that, though. I need to figure out who I'm gonna be first."

"Huh?"

My phone dings right then. I quickly pry it from the pocket of my tight jeans and look at the screen, but it isn't a message from Danny. It's just another hit on my dating app— my forty-second hit this week. I roll my eyes and toss my phone at the counter, annoyed.

"Who you're gonna be …?" Jonathan shrugs. "Your badass self. Who else?"

"This isn't just another weekend lay. Danny is different. Danny is … special." I bite my lip and stare at the floor, lost. "I don't want to mess things up. It's enough that he seems okay after what I did to him a year ago, with that kiss and everything. This is a second chance … and probably my last."

Jonathan has since learned the whole story. "Wait, you're still hung up on that? No, no, no. You're not going down *that* road again."

I frown at him. "What do you mean?"

"We don't do that anymore. We don't *pine* after people. People pine after *us*. Didn't we agree we'd *never* put ourselves in that kind of vulnerable place again?"

"I'm not *pining*."

"And now you're lying to yourself. I can see the little gross hearts in your eyes, Romeo."

I huff. "I don't just want to 'win' this guy, like another notch on the headboard. I want him more than that. I told you about Danny. And now …" I stare at the floor, as if realizing it all over again. "Now he's single. Now it could happen."

Jonathan considers me for a moment. Then he nods. "Alright. You want to go through with this, but also keep up all the progress you've made, right? I got the solution. You remember what his ex was like? That Joey asshole? Be like him. Danny is obviously into it."

I wrinkle my face up. "Into it?"

"Yeah. Considering the way you said he reacted at the gym today, seems like he enjoys being treated a little rough. He's into jerks. Maybe that's why he was with Joey for so long. He needs a guy to keep him in line. A bad boy. A dick."

"Okay, I don't think—"

"Don't change one damned thing about you. Hey." He leans forward. "You can't forget who we were a year ago— and what we are now. Don't slip back on me, buddy. There's a reason this worked out for us. I mean, look at our lives. We can have a new lay every night if we wanted. Here, in an hour with a tap of a finger, snap, you're getting laid tonight. We're the ones who get seen at the clubs. We're the ones who get the attention now. It's fucking fate." He spreads his hands. "There's a reason your special guy came back into your life at this point. He didn't show up because he's ready for you. He showed up because *you're* finally ready for *him*. You're now the man he wants."

I stare at the floor. "Not so sure."

"Oh, you'll feel sure soon enough—once you've got his clothes on your bedroom floor." Jonathan smirks at me. "Just show him how much of a dick you can really be. He'll be hard for you in no time."

I squint suspiciously at him. "You really make me wonder sometime if your whole 'I'm straight' thing is just an act. You're way too comfortable talking about hard dicks."

"So? You're my pal. We've seen each other naked. Just let me be happy for you." Jonathan glances at his phone, then hops off the counter. "Almost time to meet up with this chick I matched with. I've got a feeling she's into kinky stuff. I'll SOS you if I get tied up or something."

"And how are you gonna accomplish that if you're tied up …?"

He reaches the door and stops. He isn't the brightest crayon. "Uh … I guess I'll …" He snorts at me. "Whatever. You focus on you, okay? Don't worry about me. Get your head in the game 'cause Friday will be here before you know it." He sees himself out.

He must be psychic, because Friday *does* arrive before I know it.

I practically blink, then I'm standing on the stoop of my place, waiting for Danny to arrive. My hands are stuffed deep into the pockets of my jeans. A tight button-down shirt, opened to the chest, hugs my frame. I've got my hair styled in the perfect way that always scores me a date. My breath is good. My facial stubble is on-point. My chest is pumped from my workout earlier.

I'm basically a fuck machine ready to knock all the air out of Danny's lungs at first sight.

"Hey there, Romeo!"

I turn.

And the sight of *him* knocks all the air out of *my* lungs.

Danny is a unique, understated, easygoing brand of gorgeousness. He's in a plain white t-shirt, half-tucked into a stylish pair of jeans I want to tear right off of him. Despite

117

being dressed down and casual, he makes his outfit seem like the thoughtful wardrobe choice of a runway model—intentional, striking, and inexplicably perfect. I want to cuddle him and fuck him at the same time. I want to make love to him in ways I didn't even know I was capable of imagining. I want to own him. I want to set him free.

I'm an instant warzone of hormones within my body—emotional bombs exploding in my heart, in my limbs, in every nerve ending and muscle.

"Danny," I breathe back. "You look so ... You look ..." I flip the switch. *Resist that cutesy urge. Be the guy he wants. Stand your ground.* I turn my smile of astonishment into a smirk. "What took your ass so long?"

He chuckles in his adorable way. "I misjudged the walk. And my beagle was a bit whiny."

"Beagle?"

"Yeah. I have a dog. Sassy is her name, because ... well, she *is*." His eyes dance down my body. "You look really great, Romeo. I see your ... fashion sense has improved. I don't want to take the credit for that, exactly," he teases, "but, well, I *did* sort of march you back up to your closet to change before we went out last time."

Is that normal? To reference something from over a year ago like it just happened yesterday?

In so many ways, it feels like it *was* just yesterday that Danny and I were standing at this exact spot, our eyes all over each other, debating how our night out was going to go. We had no idea the bomb I was about to drop on him—a bomb in the form of a kiss I should never have given.

None of that comes out. I lift my chin and smirk at him. "Except *unlike* last time," I say, "you aren't taking me out to score a piece of meat. You *are* the piece of meat."

He opens his mouth, then claps it shut, staring at me.

I suffer a sudden moment of internal screaming.

Was that too far?

Then Danny laughs, breaking the tension. "That's one way to look at it! Though, uh … just to clarify something about tonight …" He leans toward me and winces as he speaks. "I just wanted to get a drink with you to chat and catch up a bit. I … wasn't really intending this to be an actual *date* … or anything."

I stare back at him, silent and stone-like.

I guess that might explain his more casual choice of attire. The old me would apologize for the misunderstanding. He'd blush and laugh it off, tell him it's okay, and go for this drink anyway, while feeling sad and frustrated the rest of the night.

The new me …

Well, I'm not sure what he'd do differently.

"Fine with me," I finally say, deciding to play it cool. "I'm down for whatever."

"Yeah? You sure?"

"Of course I'm sure."

Danny glances off for a second, then seems to make a decision. "Well, in that case, are you hungry?"

I lift an eyebrow. "Hungry? Always."

His face brightens. "Good. I've got the perfect place for us to catch up."

It's a decent walk across a noisy town full of busy streets and traffic. Holding a conversation worth anything is impossible, so we spend most of the time trying not to get run over or knocked in the face by a passerby. Soon, we're in front of a quirky-looking Asian-fusion restaurant sitting across the street from the city park. Apparently they serve the best dim sum that Danny can't get enough of, as well as some other tasty foods. We are seated at a secluded booth by the window overlooking the park. After putting in our order, we're left to stare at each other and pretend there isn't an elephant sitting on the table between us.

"So, are you—" he starts.

"I need a—" I say at the same time.

We both stop.

Then we laugh.

"I was gonna ask if you're still working in that building," he says.

"I was gonna say I need a drink. Alcohol. Something hard."

Danny chuckles. "Regretting not going to a bar instead? Trust me, once you have a taste of the *siumaai* here—the most ridiculously yummy pork and mushroom dumplings in town—you won't even remember us almost going to a bar. Did you know the term dim sum comes from *tim sam* which means 'touch the heart' in Cantonese? It's because the small portions are meant to touch the heart, not sate the appetite."

I gnaw on my lip, my foot bouncing in place impatiently.

I want to touch a lot more than just his heart right now.

"The way they make the dumplings here is the closest to

how my mom made them for me growing up. You'll want ten orders the moment you take the first bite, I'm telling you. Sorry, I ramble when I'm hungry. Oh, they *do* have a nice selection of hot teas here." He pulls a menu out of the centerpiece, sandwiched between a napkin dispenser and bottles of various sauces, and gives it a quick glance.

With each second he looks it over, I grow more restless. There are a million questions I want to ask, and even more things I want to say. What is it about him that completely disarms me like this? Shouldn't this be easy?

The only crutch I have is my attitude.

Maybe Jonathan is right. Maybe the secret is just toughing this out. Being the guy Danny wants. Being the new me—unapologetically.

"Hmm. Not as much of a selection as I remember," he complains, frowning at the menu. "Do you even drink hot tea?"

"Not usually."

"I'll find something you'll like." He starts tapping on the back of the menu with his fingers, determined.

I kick back, throwing my arms over the back of my side of the booth and spreading my legs under the table.

That results in my foot knocking into his.

His fingers stop tapping the menu.

I guess he noticed.

With a smirk, I give his foot another tap, more deliberately this time.

He ignores it, returning to drumming his fingers on the menu.

"What?" I tease him. "Don't want to play footsy with me?"

He looks up from the menu and shoots me a look.

I touch his foot with mine, then stroke it slowly with the tip of my shoe, up and down, while staring at him from across the table.

For a second, he appears to suppress a laugh. Then his face tightens. "What are we? Children?"

My lips curl upward mischievously as my foot slowly teases up to his ankle. Then I dare to slowly draw soft circles on his calf, still kicked back in my booth seat, lazily surveying my date with a foot.

I don't care what he insists this little outing of ours is. It isn't just to catch up.

He's scoping me.

And I'm scoping him.

And I'm pretty damned sure we both like what we see.

"Find anything yet?" I ask him pointedly.

"Have *you?*" he sasses back.

I innocently lift my eyebrows. "What do you mean?"

Finally, he cracks a smile. "Maybe we'll skip tea." He sets down the menu. "You like toying with me? Are you hoping I feed you dumplings and rub your feet for you?"

Wow. He really doesn't forget anything, does he? "Not at the same time," I joke back.

He tilts his head slightly and gives me an appraising look. "Not to burst your footsy flirt bubble happening underneath this table," he says, setting the drink menu aside, "but I really was serious about just wanting to chat and catch up."

I frown at him.

This wasn't the reaction I expected.

When the server comes by, I drop my foot to the floor. Our steaming-hot order of pork dumplings, rolled rice noodles, and barbecue pork buns now fill the table, as well as a basket of sticky wings. After the server leaves, the steam coming from the bowls creates a veil between me and Danny through which we stare each other down.

He smiles. "Let's dig in."

And so we do.

Danny wasn't kidding; every bite I take is better than the last. The pork dumplings transport me and every taste bud in my mouth to another dimension of sweet and salty heaven. I can't help but moan as I enjoy the rice noodles, which Danny explains are called *cheong fan,* as well as the succulent *char siu bao*—the barbecue pork buns. Where has this place been my whole life?

When we get to the wings, I quickly realize there's just no easy way to eat them. That is made perfectly clear the moment Danny grabs his first one and starts devouring it. I think with any other guy, the spark would probably go straight out as I watch my date make a mess of his face and hands eating wings covered in sticky sauce. It's like a two-year-old trying to figure out the puzzle of fitting a whole chocolate cake in their mouth.

But Danny makes it normal. Adorable, even. This could be our hundredth date, and these sweet, endearing moments could be our life together.

Except this isn't a date, remember?

He's on his second wing before I've even started my first. He's enjoying them so much, he only just now notices. "You gonna eat? They'll get cold."

I cross my arms on the table and smirk at him. "I'm having too much fun watching you."

Danny quirks an eyebrow, then frowns. "I've got sauce on my face, huh?"

He does. A tiny dot right by his lip. Another on his chin. I kinda don't want to tell him. "Nope."

"You sure?"

I lean forward. "Are you sure this isn't a date?"

He stops chewing. "Yes," he says. "This isn't a date."

"Then why don't I believe you?"

"I don't know. Ask yourself." He resumes eating.

I decide to let my foot resume asking the questions. It was doing so well a second ago. This time, I kick off my shoe and bring my socked foot to his leg, where it slowly starts to slide up, up, up, making its way to his inner thigh.

His chewing stops. He stares at me across the table, his fingers full of sauce, those two cute dots of flavor still clinging to his chin and the side of his lip.

I lift an innocent eyebrow. "What?"

He swallows his bite. "You know what."

"Just admit it."

"Admit what?"

"You're into me."

His lips part, for a moment appearing indignant. Then he snorts as he goes for another wing. "Well, that's kinda presumptuous of you, don't you think?"

"Is it, though? You were giving me all the right signs at the gym, checking me out. You asked me out on this date."

"Again, not a date," he says, his mouth full.

"And I dare you to tell me you don't like where my foot's going." I slide it farther up his inner thigh, smirking. "You like all of this, don't you? The fact that we've reunited. That we're out together again. Alone together. With nothing in the way." My foot reaches his crotch, where it stops. "*No one* in the way."

Danny stares back at me.

"Admit you're into me," I tell him, "and I might stop torturing you."

"Romeo ..."

My foot presses more firmly into his crotch, where I make a discovery through the thin material of his pants: he's hard. *Rock* hard.

I nod with admiration. "Seems like you don't have to admit it. Your cock is doing all the talking."

"This isn't a date. We're eating dim sum and wings. Well, *I* am at least."

"I don't think you're being honest with yourself. C'mon, Danny. We used to be so open with each other. Don't you want me? Isn't that why we're here?"

Danny snorts and shakes his head, either trying not to laugh or struggling to keep his composure. "I think your questions would be a lot easier to answer without your foot where it is."

"On your dick, you mean?"

"Precisely."

"You shouldn't go so long without any release, you know. Makes you too pent-up." I give a gentle nudge with my heel to his throbbing cock, causing him to grimace. "Sounds like no one's looking out for your needs. Not even yourself."

"You're trying too hard."

His words stop me. I give him a look. "What?"

"I said you're trying too hard."

I study him across the table, trying to figure out whether we're still playing or not.

All with my foot still pressed to his crotch.

"I'm looking out for my 'needs' just fine," he then says— using air quotes with his saucy fingers. "But I'm thinking the guy who hasn't been looking out for his needs is *you*."

"Huh?"

"What are you doing, anyway? Trying to impress me? Turn me on? Honestly, it's kind of cute, seeing you try so hard." He chuckles. "If not a tad annoying."

Cute? Annoying? Chuckling at me?

I'm completely at a loss.

He starts licking off his fingers while eyeing me across the table. "Romeo, the way to my heart isn't through your foot … or my dick, no matter how it's reacting. I'm a dude. It's been a while. I can't help it if it gets stiff. I'll tell you one thing though, this isn't the way to win me over."

I glower at him. "So should I just give up, then?" I grunt as he goes for another wing. "Is that what you're saying?"

"Nope. Just saying what you're doing now is *so* not working." He takes a bite, then eyes me. "But you should definitely keep trying."

I quirk an eyebrow.

Keep trying ...?

"Good," he decides, even though I didn't say anything. "Now that *that's* out of the way, can we be two grown men on an outing tonight without turning this all sexual? I really *was* hungry, as is evidenced by my shameless face-stuffing, and wanted to share my favorite dim sum with you. I also do still want to catch up some." He nods at the basket. "You gonna try some of these before I eat them all?"

It's like he's immune to me suddenly. What my foot is pressed up against might as well be the tough and impenetrable iron codpiece to some medieval knight's armor. Or a goddamned chastity device. I have no hope of getting through.

I drop my foot to the floor, my eyes as sharp as darts as I stare at him.

Danny nudges the basket my way, then winks. "Try one. They're finger-lickin' good."

I'm already staring at something that's finger-licking good. He's sitting across the table from me, not letting me lick one damned inch of him.

If he thinks I'm ever gonna stop trying to win him over, he's finger-lickin' wrong.

14. Weak

WE STROLL THROUGH THE CALM PARK ACROSS THE STREET, bright white streetlamps lighting the path. Our hands are in our pockets, and the conversation is mild and occasionally broken by long, contemplative silences. We stop at the duck pond and stare out at the water for some time.

If this was any other date, he'd be bent over a piece of furniture in my apartment by now.

I've been going so fast over the past year, I don't know if I can handle this excruciatingly slow pace. Am I even capable of it? Or have I lost the ability to hold a simple fucking conversation? Is all I am just a bunch of flirty one-liners to get the guy to my place, then sex-sex-sex until I show them the door?

"What're you thinking about?"

I flinch, startled from my thoughts. "Hmm? What?"

"You're somewhere else." Danny chuckles as he observes me. "I'm just wondering what's on your mind. Anything you care to share?"

Light reflects off the water from the nearby light posts

and dances across his face, now and then catching in his eyes and causing them to sparkle.

For one split second, I'm about to throw some quip about how all I've got on my mind is wondering how he looks like naked and picturing us skinny-dipping in that pond doing every last nasty thing we can imagine.

Then just as quickly, I picture us sitting on a bench by that shimmering pond, sharing a tender moment, our hearts aflutter, before getting lost in one another's eyes and sharing a meaningful kiss.

"Bet you're thinking about all that tasty dim sum."

I give him a look. Then I snort and play along. "You bet." I gaze at the side of his face, trying not to look too hopelessly enamored. "It's all I'm thinking about."

Actually, the food *was* pretty damned good, but that sure as hell isn't what's consuming me right now. He knows it, too.

"Really, you can tell me," he says. "Whatever it is that's on your mind. Even if it's something weird. Like you're wondering if you forgot to water your plant on your windowsill. Or maybe left a lamp on in your apartment."

I smile, recalling that night, and eye him. "You mean the moody, atmospheric lamp I'm supposed to leave on in case I bring a date back?"

He appears impressed. "You remembered."

"I'd never forget."

Danny glances down at the ground. I wonder if his mind is going somewhere too now. Then he lifts his eyes to mine. "And how's your plant?"

"Dead."

He gasps. "Oh, I'm sorry to hear that! It ... It was such a pretty plant."

"It was around my birthday last year. Just sort of ... started shriveling up, nothing I did seemed to revive it. Seems on par with things I care about." I shrug. "Guess I'm not so good at taking care of things other than myself after all. Bad first impression for potential *boyfriends*."

"Hey, don't beat yourself up too much about it. Taking care of a plant can be hard work," he points out. "Especially considering the plant."

"Or the boyfriend." I turn to him. "Am I the reason you and Joey broke up?"

The question stops him completely. He looks at me. We're both frozen in place, our eyes intensely connected as if by a steel cable.

I follow my unanswered question with another: "What did you tell Joey? About what happened that night? You had to have told him something. He came at me in the gym."

"I ..." His whole face changes. "Wait, he what?"

"Was he mad? When you told him?"

"I mean ..." He glances down at the water, as if to find the memory. "He wasn't *not* mad. But he was always a bit hard to read whenever he got angry. He would stuff things down all the time, then pick the absolute worst moment to blow up. Like halfway through a rewatch of my favorite movie on Christmas Eve, for example. Or on my birthday." He looks me in the eye. "Why are you asking this?"

"It's something that's on my mind. Since you asked."

He frowns. "And he 'came at you in the gym' you said?"

"Yep. Pinned me to a wall. I was half turned on. It was confusing."

Danny bites his lip with frustration. "It's all the more reason to have broken it off with him when I did." He looks at me. "I'm sorry, Romeo. I didn't mean for that to happen."

"I guess he was just being protective of you. It makes sense." I stop. *Wait, am I actually defending that prick?*

Danny notices, too. "That's rather … understanding of you."

I shrug. "I mean, the guy's still a fucking tool, don't get me wrong."

"I'm still sorry it happened."

"I'm not sorry for *why* it happened."

Danny turns to me. He seems like he was about to say something, but my words stopped him.

I take a step closer to Danny. "The difference between that night and tonight … is now we're both single. And alone."

Feeling brave, I bring a hand to the side of his head, giving his hair a gentle stroke as I peer into his eyes. His breathing changes. Mine, too. I can't remember the last time I felt this vulnerable to someone.

Actually, I do. It was when he put his hand through my hair. Just like this. "You have some perfect hair, too, y'know," I tell him, echoing his words thoughtfully. "Always falls into a style, no matter what you do with it. Easy to … just run your fingers through it."

Danny gets lost in my eyes, speechless.

He's captured. I've got him. I remember every detail about that night, and I know he does, too. My hand slides to the back of his head, where I gently take hold. I slowly bring my face toward his, closing my eyes, ready for his lips to meet mine again.

My mouth meets a finger instead.

I open my eyes, confused, to find him pressing a finger to my lips.

"Not so fast, Smooth Moves," he says.

"I thought we were having a moment," I mumble against his finger.

"Tonight's going great so far, isn't it?"

"I … yeah, it is, but—"

"So why ruin it with a kiss?"

"Since when has a kiss ruined anything? Kisses are the best," I say, my lips still pressed to his finger. "You know what I think? I think you're hot for me and won't admit it. I think …" I take his finger and gently move it out of the way. "… you're wondering how that night would have gone if you weren't with Joey at the time."

His eyes drop to my lips.

"Here's your chance, Danny. It's just us. This whole night is ours. You're feeling it. I'm feeling it. So kiss me. Just give in and kiss me."

I feel the sexual tension tightening between us. It's unmistakable. Like a powerful fucking magnet, pulling our bodies closer and closer.

My lips have to be his first and last thought.

His lips are my only destination.

We're just one figurative nudge away from at last seeing where this night can go.

All I need to do is—

"You're charming, Romeo."

I blink. "What?"

"Charming." A smile touches his lips, and his eyes sparkle curiously. "Underneath all of this smooth-talking, I still see the sweet guy whose gym membership I renewed ... even though I suspect you wasted most of that membership since you stopped going," he teases, then he meets my eyes. "But I don't want the charming Romeo. I want the real Romeo, the one that all of this charm is trying to cover up."

"I *am* the real Romeo. These are my ... my real feelings, and ... I'm not trying to cover ..." But the rest of that sentence dies on my parted lips. Is he right? Am I still doing my usual routine, treating him like I do my casual dates, inching our inevitable way to a bedroom?

He takes a step back from me. "Obviously I like you, Romeo. That's why I want to take this slow."

"I'm not just 'smooth talking', you know."

"That's why I'm still spending time with you tonight."

"Even the ducks in that pond want us to make out, for fuck's sake."

"... and that's why I kissed you back."

I meet his eyes. Those last words did something to his face, like he finally let go of something he was clinging to since the start of the night—something he was holding back.

"That night, long ago," he says. "That night was magical. From diving into your closet, to accidentally giving you a boner, to falling on the floor of that bar and kissing you over a pile of your cash and credit cards. Timing ... wasn't on our side then, but we have it now, and I don't want to rush it. I respect you too much to do that. So ... for now, I just want us to be friends, okay?"

Friends.

Fuck me, did he really just say that?

Impatience floods my system. With every desperate beat of my heart, I just want to grab him and make him mine. I want to catch up for lost time. I want to do everything to him that I couldn't that night long ago.

And my own date is cock blocking me.

Is that the point? Denial? Holding back? Going slow? Is this really what he wants?

Maybe that's exactly what I should have been doing since the start.

Driving him crazy.

Making him want me more.

"Alright," I reluctantly manage to say, taking a step back as well. "I can respect ... your wishes. We can take this slow. Super slow." My eyes drag down his body. I swallow back my frustration. "As slow as you want."

He lifts an eyebrow. "Really?"

"Yep." My cock might bust out of my pants right now. My heart wants to leap out of my chest and jump into his. My hands want to rip off every thread of his clothes that hide his sexy body. "You and me. Just friends. Really."

Despite my reassurances, a glint of suspicion burns in his eyes. "You sure?"

"Totally, absolutely, one-hundred percent sure." I force my hands into my pockets, despite their own wishes. "In fact, I won't make another move until you're absolutely ready. After all, like you so kindly reminded me at the restaurant, we're only catching up tonight, right? This isn't an actual date, so no pressure."

"Right. No ..." He fidgets. "... no pressure."

No pressure, yet it's obvious we both feel a ton of it.

In our pants.

I nod slowly despite the challenge. He wants to take it slow? Oh, I'll take it slow, then. Really slow. *Two can play this game, baby.*

15. Hard-To-Get

WEIGHTS CRASH TO THE FLOOR.

A single droplet of sweat makes its way from my forehead to the tip of my nose.

I lie back on the bench, then start another set.

"Alright, Romeo. Are you gonna tell me how the date went? Or are you gonna keep anger-lifting?" asks Jonathan.

I drop my weights to the ground with a growl, then go to the rack for something heavier. I return and resume my workout, huffing.

He watches from the bench next to me. "That bad, huh?"

I ignore him as I keep pumping away.

"Yikes. I guess you went home with a case of blue balls, huh?"

"Blue doesn't cover it," I finally manage to groan as I struggle to make the last rep, my arms shaking, veins popping, before finally dropping the weights to the floor with a sigh, breathing deeply.

Jonathan comes around in front of me. "Did you do what we talked about?"

"I did. Your advice was terrible. The date went totally wrong."

"Seriously?"

"Yep. And that's exactly why I've got it in the bag." I sit up. "I'm gonna win Danny's heart." I pick up the weights again and start another set.

Now Jonathan is truly confused. "Huh?"

"He wants to play hard-to-get?" I laugh between reps. "Two can play. I'll let the sexual tension swell. I'll let him drool over me every benign date we go on. Drive him crazy. Never give in to my own instincts. Hold out as long as humanly possible." I grin as I drop my weights again. "It's genius."

"How is that even remotely genius?"

I turn to him. "Because I'm gonna force *him* to make the first move."

"Uh ..."

"By the time he finally *does* cave—which is inevitable— he is going to cave *so hard*, we'll probably have sex for a week straight. It's obvious he wants me. And can you blame him? I'm not the guy I was a year ago. He's about to learn that the hard way." I smirk victoriously. "The *very, ragingly hard* way."

"This sounds like a terrible plan."

"It's the most terrible plan I've ever made." I set my weights down. "And that's exactly why it'll work."

Jonathan shakes his head. "That ... sounds like the fucking *opposite* of what you should be doing. You should be getting laid nightly, man. It's the only way you can deal. Is this Danny guy really worth it?"

I turn to him. *He's the only guy who's worth it.* But for some reason, I just say, "Yeah, his ass is that hot. And it's the last ass in this town I haven't tapped yet."

He chuckles at that, then resumes his workout.

And I stare at the mirror across from me, for a moment not recognizing the guy staring back. To be honest, I don't think I've had sex with as many men as I make it seem like to Jonathan. I mean, sure, the amount of sexual partners I've had has increased tenfold since last year, but considering the abysmal lack of a sex life I had before, that's not saying much. People look at me more. I get a dozen dings on my dating app a day—and that might even be putting it modestly. And I have no fears or insecurities here at the gym anymore. Everything about me is different. Even my best friend is new. I've literally traded my life for a completely new one.

Yet sometimes, when I catch eyes with the guy in the mirror, it feels like all of this is just some weird, demented dream I'll someday wake up from. Like this is not really me. Like I was a fool to ever think it was.

Until I hear: "Hey there, Romeo."

I turn my head. Danny stands next to my bench in his workout gear: tight tank, tiny gym shorts that glorify the gift of his shapely, toned legs, sporty socks that go halfway up his baseball calves, and Nike sneakers. When he smiles at me, the whole world washes away, and all I know is the pitter-patter of my ridiculously tortured heart.

I ignore that pitter-patter and shoot him a smirk. "Hey there yourself, hot shot."

"Anyway, I just wanted to say hi, and ... tell you I had a great time last night."

I feel Jonathan staring hardcore at the side of my face, as if egging me on. I give Danny the sweetest smile I can muster. "Me too. Mind if I go ahead and finish my set?"

"Oh, right. Don't want to interrupt your workout. I should go and ..." He chuckles, blushes, then nods at the weights. "... get sweaty."

"Have fun ... *friend*." I shoot him another casual smile, then resume my set.

You know. As if Danny isn't the center of my whole fucking universe.

He hesitates, as if wanting to say something else, then decides against it and goes to the rack. I pay his cute ass absolutely no mind as I lie back and continue to grunt out some more sets. Jonathan shakes his head, likely having no idea what to make of my tactic, and continues his own workout.

I have full confidence in my plan.

But that doesn't mean it's easy.

Especially when Danny starts grunting at a bench near mine, and it does everything to pull my focus. At one point, I nearly drop a dumbbell on my foot as my hopeless eyes glue to Danny's arms as they flex and pump with his every muscular effort. It's impossible *not* to watch. Before he notices my ogling, I quickly slap shut my mouth and snap back to attention on my own workout.

This is me, doubling down on self-denial.

It's going to work, I insist.

Then moments later, I'm sitting at the fly machine doing my reps, minding my own business, when Danny sits at the machine across the aisle from me. He gives me a mild smile of acknowledgement, then starts doing bicep curls. We've both got ear buds in, our brains being blasted with whatever playlists we've got going on, yet there always seems to be this invisible tunnel between us. I can't do anything without him noticing. He can't do anything without me being finely aware of every last movement he makes.

Someone walks past us—a gorgeous hunk of a man, who glances at me over his shoulder. His eyes linger far too long to be casual. He gives me a greeting in the form of a chin-lift and a wink.

Danny notices.

As this is also a secret part of my plan, I return the guy's greeting with a nod of my own—plus a smirk for good measure—then return to my workout. I'm not looking at Danny, but I can feel every inch of him on fire as he stares at me.

Then I'm at the chest press machine, pushing for dear life, as Danny is bent over the bench of the leg curl machine, pumping his hamstrings. And with each rep, his tight, glorious ass keeps lifting slightly off of the bench, like a goddamned invitation, distracting me. Which muscle group is he targeting today? Is it leg *and* arm day for him? Or is he just using that machine to distract the fuck out of me? I clench my teeth and work out, my eyes trapped by the sight of his firm, flexing cheeks. When he finishes, he steps off the machine and glances my way—only I'm quicker and pretend to be staring off, bobbing my head to the music in my ears.

And I'm just in time for another pair of guys to walk past me, and both of them stop their chatting to look my way. One gives a little wave. I nod back, smirking as they strut by. I feel Danny's eyes on me the whole time—which is the point—and I let him exude waves of jealousy as I pretend to check out those guys' asses as they walk away.

It's going to work, I keep insisting—even still.

Then we both end up at the water dispenser together, side-by-side. He gives me a smile. I return it with a cool one of my own before refilling my bottle from the machine. Some toned and slender guy comes behind me. I make a big show of noticing him checking out my ass, then grab my filled bottle and give him a wink as I walk off. Danny watches. If his expression was troubled earlier, it's nothing compared to the near-panicked look in his sweet eyes now.

Is he wondering yet if his own plan to "take things slow" was a dumpster fire of a bad idea?

Especially considering all of the attention the 'new me' gets now.

A fuck-ton of attention the 'old me' certainly never got.

In time, I'm in the locker room changing out of my sweaty gym clothes. Jonathan is nearby trying to work out a knot in his shoelaces, when I notice Danny approaching a locker nearby. I give him his due attention—which is just a mild glance and a smile—before peeling off my shirt. Danny stares at my shirtless bod, perhaps taken aback by how much it's changed in a year. Knowing I have his attention, I take my gym shirt and make a slow, nearly pornographic show of wiping the sweat off of my body. I dab under my pits. I rub the shirt down my front. I even start stretching my arms as if to work out a few kinks in my muscles, taking my sweet-ass time being shirtless and acting like I don't notice Danny ogling me with a desperately thirsty look in his eyes.

Drink it in, stud.

"You have a good workout?"

I turn. Danny has come up to my side. He's a total fucking vision himself—freshly pumped, veins in his slender biceps, hair slightly matted from his efforts. I can barely focus on his words.

But I do. I'm determined not to let a single drop of figurative drool fall from my lips. "Yep."

"That's great." He appears uncomfortable for a second before adding, "I definitely noticed you get a lot of attention here at this gym."

I smirk. "Yeah, happens all the time."

"All the time?"

"Can't help it if guys flock to me." I shrug as I fetch my clean shirt out of the locker. "I'm sure you're used to being noticed, yourself."

"Well ..." He chuckles again. His eyes are all over me. This has to be driving him crazy. "I guess I just never noticed them before."

Of course not. You only concerned yourself with all of the eyes on *me*. "You never do."

He lifts an eyebrow. "What do you mean?"

"You never seem to give yourself enough credit for how gorgeous you are."

Then I freeze.

I didn't mean to let that slip out.

"Anyway," I quickly go on, talking over the sudden drumming of my heart—and the look Danny is giving me right now, "I gotta get home and take a shower." I thrust my shirt on, slam shut the locker too fast, then sling my backpack over a shoulder. "See you around, Danny. Later, Jonathan." I push through the doors of the locker room.

I barely reach the exit of the gym when I hear Danny call at my back. "Hey, Romeo?"

I stop and turn.

Danny comes up to me. His face scrunches up as he gathers his words. "So, uh, I was ... There's this thing ..." He clears his throat, meets my eyes, and tries again. "I was wondering if you wanted to join me for this ... little hangout thing I'm going to tomorrow night around eight-ish? Some of my coworkers are gathering at our boss's place—this high-rise condo across town—for a few drinks, maybe a movie, or just hanging out and having fun. I never know what to expect at my boss's place." He laughs self-consciously, then lifts his eyebrows. "I hate going alone every time. I was ... wondering if you'd like to be my plus-one."

Play it cool.

Keep it casual.

You've got him in your palm.

"And ... we're going as friends to this thing?" I ask.

"Of course," he answers too quickly, fidgets, then smiles. "Yes. So do you wanna go with me?"

"You bet your ass I'll be your plus-one," I answer—with

a touch more enthusiasm than intended.

He smiles that heart-crushingly beautiful smile I can't get enough of. "Great. I'm taking a taxi there, so ... I'll stop by your place around 7:45 to pick you up, since it's on the way." He seems confused about what else to say for a moment, then finally settles on: "See you then, Romeo." With that, he heads back to the locker room—and my eyes drop straight to his tiny gym shorts, instantly hypnotized by Danny's firm, tight cheeks squeezed inside them as he struts away.

Fuck.

Maybe it's me who's in his palm.

16. Friends?

THE TAXI PULLS UP PROMPTLY AT 7:45 PM. I POP OPEN THE door, slip inside, then Danny and I head off across town. He asks me how my day at work was. I ask him about his boss and whether he's a dick like mine, and he explains that *she* is actually very nice and is a little obsessed with gay men, hence why she seems to only hire them, befriend them, and totally surround herself with them. He compliments my outfit with carefully chosen words and tries not to stare at me too long. I ask if he's wearing cologne and try not to sound too much like I want to tackle him. He starts warning me about his coworkers and what I should expect when we get there.

All of it is small talk.

All of it is blah, blah, blah.

It's obvious all he wants to do right now is ditch the get together and beg me to fuck his brains out in the back seat of this smelly taxi.

Tonight is going to be so much fun torturing him.

We arrive on-time—and this is no modest high-rise building. Just from the look of the lobby, I got the fast

145

impression that this place is luxurious. There was a handsomely-dressed concierge who greeted us downstairs. There were elevator attendants and security guards. Even the elevators talk to you as you ascend. By the time we get to the door of his boss's apartment, my eyes are full of gold and glam.

I turn to him. "Is your boss mega loaded or something?"

Danny seems more fidgety than normal as we stand at the door to the high-rise apartment, waiting to be let in. "She's my boss, but she also owns the whole chain of stores I work at. I probably should've mentioned that. She's a big deal."

"No shit." The walls tremble with the sound of chatter, laughter, and music thumping at top volume. I give him a nudge of my elbow. "And, uh ... didn't you say this was a small gathering ...?"

He clears his throat. "Um, yeah."

What's going on? "You alright, Danny?"

"Sorry, what?"

"I asked if you're alright."

He takes a breath. "Okay. I might have, uh ... downplayed my boss Denise's parties. They can go from a 'little get-together' to a huge event in minutes."

"That," I say, pointing, "sounds like a full-blown ticketed event with a DJ and mosh pit through that door."

"I ... also ... might have told my boss I was bringing a friend." He winces. "And that may have resulted in a group text going out to some of her *other* gay friends. And *their* friends. And my *coworkers'* friends. I guess she can go a little over the top." He sighs. "I have no idea what we're about to face in there."

"They'd make all of that fuss just over you bringing a friend?" Danny makes a face. I lean in. "What exactly did you tell them about me?"

"Nothing."

He's lying. "Did you tell your boss how we met? Or that I'm the reason you broke it off with Joey?"

Danny's face is going red. He shoots me a look. "You're *not* the reason."

"Did you tell your boss I'm hot?"

Now his face is a literal cherry. He rolls his eyes and suppresses a laugh. "You think pretty damned highly of yourself, huh?"

I fight an instinct to tell him he doesn't have to worry, that the only guy I have eyes for is him, no matter how many hotties and party-boy horn dogs are on the other side of this door. The whole point of this 'hard-to-get' thing is to drive Danny crazy and make *him* pursue *me* when he's ready, right?

But maybe he could use some reassurance anyway. *Just a little bit.* "Danny ..."

Just then, the door flings open, and a vibrant, curvy woman in a cocktail dress appears. She has dark, tight curls of hair, warm mahogany skin, and bright green eyes that flash upon seeing us. "Danny, you're here, my sweetheart! And, oh my ..." She turns to me with a hand full of stylish jewelry drawn to her chest—then proceeds to take in the sight of me like I'm a delicious slab of prime beef. "This must be your ... friend ...?"

"Yes, ma'am." Danny nervously presents me with a gesture, like I'm a magic trick. "This is Romeo. Romeo, this is Denise."

When she smiles, her eyes glow like green embers. "Mmm, the more the merrier. Come inside, you two! Just about everyone's here already, plus a few more, and there is *so* much to eat." Her gaze falls on me again. "It's *oh-so-nice* to meet you, Romeo."

I smile back.

It isn't the last thirsty welcome I receive.

When I enter, I am overwhelmed at once by music, flashy lighting, and a *lot* of eye contact. The place is luxurious and humungous, decorated from floor to ceiling like a damned night club. The condo is packed with mostly men, and a few women sprinkled throughout the crowd. There's an enormous spread of food, a DJ playing music, and some kind of light display throwing colors and lasers all over the ceiling.

What in ritzy disco hell have I just wandered into?

Denise ushers me in so fast, I lose sight of Danny in seconds. A rather eclectic assortment of faces surround me with greetings. "Uh, hey," I say to one face, before being instantly swept away by another. "Hi, I'm Romeo," I greet someone else. "Yes, I'm Danny's friend. Romeo," I answer another. "Romeo, right, like the play." Over and over. "Yep, Danny brought me." And over. "Romeo's the name. Hi."

The women at this party are far and few between, but they're there, and even they have eyes for me, like they're wondering just how far my pendulum swings, and whether it might include one of them some wild night.

148

I don't even get this much attention at the places I hit up with Jonathan.

Through a slim hole in the crowd, I spot Danny in the kitchen with Denise, the pair of them equipped with glasses of wine already. Danny glances my way, a nervous glint in his eyes. He smiles tentatively.

I smile back.

Then a freckly, rosy-cheeked face appears, blocking my view of Danny. "Hey there, Rome, sir," he says.

I blink. Wait a sec …

"Do you remember me?" he asks. "I rubbed your feet in a movie theater and fed you popcorn."

Fuck me. It's Benjamin-Benny-Bradley-Brian. "Uh …"

"It's Tim. My name."

Uh, okay, way off. "Yeah. I remember you."

"Cool. You look like you gained a lot of muscle since the last time I saw you. Have you become more dominant, too?"

"I dunno. More of an asshole, really." I peer around his head for Danny, but only barely catch a glimpse of him gazing my way with curiosity before I lose sight of him again.

"I like that, Rome, sir. Maybe we can catch another movie sometime. Or just skip all the boring stuff and go back to my place. Or yours. Do you own rope? Or a ball-gag at the very least? I like more things now."

Everyone is in the way. I'm drowning in a sea of mindless conversation. "Sure, whatever."

This is really not the person I want to be stuck talking to right now. The point of tonight isn't to meet Danny's coworkers or my past dating nightmares. It's to continue executing my plan with Danny until he is ready to become all mine.

I finally manage to regain sight of the kitchen—only to find Danny gone. Where'd he go?

"Hmm. Not as much enthusiasm as I'd like, but I can manage. I haven't had much luck lately in the love department, I guess. Well, as much luck as you can have in such a department when it isn't love you're looking for. Not exactly, anyway."

I need to find Danny. All of this is pointless if he isn't witnessing it. "Get me a drink and wait for me in the kitchen."

Tim lifts his eyebrows, instantly converted to an excited puppy. "Oh, really? That's your order?"

"Yep. I gotta find my friend."

With that—and before waiting for any response from Tim—I slip away through the crowd, looking for Danny. Did his boss take him off to gossip about me? Why is this place so damned big, yet so damned crowded?

The next thing I know, another face I half-recognize is in front of me, blocking the way. "Oh my god, it *is* you."

I look at him, confused. No bells ring. "Sorry?"

"We went out. Maybe a month or two ago. Then I never heard from you again."

"Sorry, must've been a different guy," I mumble, then scoot around him and continue my pursuit.

Until another pair of men drinking cocktails by the couch spot me. "Hey, don't I know you?" one of them asks, squinting at me. Then his eyes light up. "Oh, right, it's you! The guy from King's who I—"

"Wait," interjects his friend. "You hooked up with him, too? So did I!" He gawps at me. "It's been a while since I— Hey, Romeo, you stud, don't run away. Come chat with us! You never returned my texts."

"Nor mine!" says his friend, and they both laugh.

Sweat is beading on my forehead. I ignore both of them and change directions, desperate to find Danny now. Everywhere I go, eyes are on me. Faces. Blank stares. Curious stares. Horny stares. I poke my head into what appears to be a windowless office, where my arrival interrupts five guys and a young woman in the middle of a heated discussion. When their stony eyes fall on me, I can't help but wonder if I'm the subject. I quickly flee that room in a heartbeat, whether or not I'm who they were talking about at all. I am intercepted no less than five more times, each person wanting to introduce themselves, or say hi, or drop some stupid flirty one-liner, or ask why I look familiar.

I guess it was bound to happen that I start running into my past hookups.

I just didn't expect it to be at a party full of Danny's goddamned coworkers and their friends.

Then I find the sliding glass door to a large open balcony, where a group has gathered around a fancy set of outdoor furniture. Yet again, my appearance seems to stop the conversation.

Except this time, Danny is among them, sitting by himself in an armchair, with Denise across from him in a love seat next to another woman. Eight guys populate the L-shaped couch—all of them peering over their shoulders at me.

"Join us, Romeo!" calls out Denise with a gesture toward the couch. "Everyone wants to get to know Danny's new friend."

I look at Danny.

He stares back at me, his face as blank as a stone. What does he know? What does he think? What is going through his head?

Is my plan working or backfiring miserably?

I join the group of curious faces, taking the one spot available: on the couch, sandwiched between two men who make very little effort to give me room. It's almost a damned cuddle-fest out here, all of these men glued to the sight of me.

It's strange, how the tables have turned from that fateful night Danny and I shared at that bar, when he was the one who earned every last single man's attention.

Now it's me.

And it only matters if it's doing the trick of making Danny reconsider his stance on taking things slow and keeping me at a distance. As my eyes remain on him, I find him gripping the arms of his chair like he's clinging to the edge of a cliff, ready to claw at the bare rock for dear life.

The questions start immediately. "So, like, you're Danny's friend from the gym, huh? Did I hear that right?"

"Yep," I answer—yet again.

"But you guys aren't … a thing …?" someone else asks.

I stare at Danny as I give my answers. "Just friends."

"Hmm." A few faces turn suggestively to Danny, smirking. "Friends? Nothing more? Really?"

I stare at Danny. After a lengthy hesitation where I give him the opportunity to answer—which he doesn't—I shrug. "Just friends."

"So in other words, you're fair game?"

A platter of finger foods rests on the glass coffee table between me and Danny. I reach forward, pluck a block of cheese, then daintily pop it into my mouth. "I guess so, huh?" I smirk at Danny, throw my arms over the back of the couch, and chew with delight.

Danny swallows hard.

This is only going to get worse for you the longer you hold out, baby.

"Well, I think that's good news to just about everyone out here," says one of my couch mates, who I will pretend isn't trying to cuddle against my side, and everyone laughs.

"Assuming he only plays for one team," puts in Denise, lifting an eyebrow.

I smile at her. "Sorry, but yeah, I only score homeruns for the boys." And everyone laughs again.

I'm apparently quite the crowd pleaser tonight.

Danny sits forward suddenly. "We met for the first time at the gym I used to work at, actually. That's where we first became friends. It was … It was fun." His face turns red as he awkwardly—and desperately—attempts to redirect the conversation somewhere less interesting. "In fact, the marketing firm he works for is actually in that same building, too, so I would see him almost every day when he and his coworkers—"

"Oh, what do you do there?" the guy to my side asks me, appearing very interested and cutting Danny off—much to his chagrin.

I shrug. "Piss off my boss, mostly." Everyone laughs. "No, seriously. All I do is get paid to piss off my boss, every day, all day. And I don't get fired. It's the best job ever. Just the other day, I basically pulled out my dick and measured it right in front of him. He obviously has a tiny penis complex, and it makes him the world's biggest douchebag. Hey," I go on over more laughter, "it's not my fault his wife doesn't put out, yet he takes it out on me anyway. Though, the last time I pissed him off, it turned into this amazing idea he ended up loving, and I swear, I almost got a promotion. Maybe that's why I've never been fired. Does he secretly like it? Me making fun of his little dick?"

I shrug to the tune of everyone continuing to laugh.

Everyone except Danny, who looks like he just swallowed a pineapple.

Especially when the guy next to me leans in, places his hand on my thigh, and says, "Oh my god, you are hilarious *and* handsome. Is this guy a unicorn or what?"

"Calm down there, Elliot," says someone from behind the couch, clutching a bottle of beer. "You sound like you're already halfway in bed with him."

The pretty-faced guy next to me with short curls of sandy blond hair and a tanned complexion—Elliot, apparently—shrugs. "I can't help it." He fixes his eyes on me. "I like what I see."

Knowing I have Danny's undivided attention, I give this Elliot guy a suggestive smirk, pretending to be totally into the flattery.

Elliot turns to Danny suddenly, his curls bouncing. "Okay, thanks for bringing him for me, Danny, so sweet of you to remember my birthday gift a month late, I'll go ahead and take Mr. Romeo home with me now to unwrap." Everyone laughs at that, including Elliot himself, who nudges me with a bony elbow and adds, "Just kidding. I wouldn't be so presumptuous. Or would I? No, really, just kidding."

I doubt there's a bone in his body that's kidding at all.

Especially the one swelling in his too-tight pants.

"Denise!" calls a voice from the glass doors. "They're playing your song!"

"Oh, oh, oh!" Denise is out of her chair. "I'm not missing it! Guys, c'mon in! Someone's gotta dance with me!"

Before I know it, everyone is relocating inside, and I get pushed along with the crowd like driftwood caught in a current. I try to find Danny over my shoulder, but once again I'm lost among cheering faces, pumping fists, and noise. Some disco song I should know the name of vibrates the room at top volume, and everyone is going ballistic.

Elliot grabs hold of my hands and starts dancing next to me. I bob my head and move a little to the music as my eyes scan the crowd for any sign of Danny. "Baby, you've got smooth moves!" cries Elliot through the noise. I pretend I can't hear him. "I like the way you dance! It's so hot!"

I'm barely dancing. I suck at it.

This guy is just horny as fuck for me, bottom line.

Finally I spot Danny. He's dancing with Denise, who looks positively in a trance as she flails her arms to the music. He glances my way, apparently knowing exactly where I am.

Now that I've got his attention, the plan snaps right back into place. I give him a smirk, then put my hands on Elliot's hips and dance along with him, getting into it. I can see the visible sting of jealousy in Danny's eyes. It's so palpable, I can literally taste it like sour candy on my tongue.

It's just a matter of time before he gives in, cuts through the crowd, and steals me away.

He'll tell me no more friend bullshit.

He'll tell me he wants me all to himself.

And I will be all for it.

But he hasn't yet. And despite how cool I'm acting about it all, it's frustrating. As Elliot gets more and more handsy—now practically grinding his hips against mine as we dance—I have to consider a few things. Danny isn't a dumb guy. He *must* know deep down what I'm doing. I've been giving him so much suggestive eye contact tonight, we've practically already fucked. I'm playing up the "we're just friends because Danny said so" bit, which is the world's biggest smoke signal for saying "I actually want to be with Danny, but the cock-teasing bastard is keeping me at arm's length". Not to mention how rather obvious and forward I was during our date.

Being just friends and taking this at a glacial pace was his idea. Bringing me here was his idea. He knows exactly what I really want, yet isn't making a move.

Is something else going on here?

Other than Elliot's hand slowly inching its way to my ass.

As the song comes to an end, everyone cheers, and the next thing I know, I've lost sight of Danny. "One sec," I say, cutting off something Elliot is telling me, and make my way through the crowd. I spot Danny slipping into the bathroom halfway down the hall, where I quickly make my way.

I open the door and let myself inside, shutting it behind me.

Danny has his pants unzipped when he spins around, startled by my arrival.

His pants drop to the floor.

I cross my arms and lean back against the door. "Well, this situation looks familiar. One of us caught with our pants down. The other fully clothed and enjoying it."

Danny's face turns red as he grabs his pants and pulls them back up. "I was trying to go to the bathroom."

"Your underwear is sexy, by the way."

His face can't get any redder. "You look like you're having a lot of fun out there with Elliot."

"He's a fun guy. Or a drunk guy. Can't tell. But I do know he likes unicorns."

"Do you mind? I gotta pee."

"Why didn't you lock the door?"

"I *really* gotta pee."

"Are we still doing this friend thing?" I ask Danny, taking a few steps forward, then leaning against the sink, right next to him, so close I can feel his warmth.

He gives me an oddly defiant look. For someone who's so sweet and kindhearted, the expression sits oddly on his face, like it doesn't belong there. "Yes," he finally answers. "We are."

I let my eyes float on his lips. I can still taste them. I can still feel their pillowy softness against my own. My heart races just from the thought. "You sure?"

"Of course. Why wouldn't I ..." He hesitates, for a second losing his own breath. "Why wouldn't I be? I said I didn't want to rush into anything, didn't I?"

I meet his eyes again. The tension between us is wire-tight and unbearable. He really wants to play this thing out, apparently—to its bitter, frustrating end.

"Now please, will you let me take a piss in peace?"

"Sure thing ... friend." Then I see myself out of the bathroom. I hear the click of the door's lock after it shuts.

Danny sure is one frustrating piece of work. Why does that make me want him even more? Is that part of his game? Is he playing out a diabolical plan of his own?

Who's playing whom?

When I make it out of the hallway, I notice Elliot in the center of the throng right away, dancing like his dick depends on it. Taking advantage of the glorious dancing distraction, I scurry along the edge of the room to the kitchen, where I intend to find myself a drink.

That's when I run into ... shit, I've already forgotten his name again. Jerry? Jim? "Uh ..."

He comes right up to me obediently, carrying a glass of wine. "Hi there, Rome, sir. I got you a drink and waited here in the kitchen, like you ordered."

To be honest, I completely forgot. "You've ... seriously

been waiting here all this time with my drink …?"

"Yes, sir."

I take the drink, then hold it awkwardly, not sipping from it. As if I needed to feel even more like the evil mastermind of my own diabolical scheme than I already do, now I have a willing minion at my bidding. I don't want to fathom what comes next.

Until suddenly what's next comes for me: Elliot, emerging from the dancing throng as a sweaty, out-of-breath hot mess. "Oh my god, Romeo, what are you doing all the way over here?" He doesn't so much as glance at Tim. *Oh, right, his name's Tim.* "You owe me a dance, mister!"

Elliot's arm slips around the small of my back as he falls against my side, like I'm already his score of the night, a sure deal, claimed.

Tim notices. "Oh. Is this your boyfriend, sir?"

Elliot looks up, noticing him for the first time. He squints, then turns to me and asks in a quiet voice: "Who's the weirdo?"

The moment my lips part to give an answer, someone else appears at my other side.

Danny.

"Oh, hey," I start to greet him.

Without a moment's hesitation, he swipes the glass of wine right out of my hand and downs the whole thing. Then he hands the glass off to Tim, lets out a surprisingly hearty burp, and faces me. "I want to dance."

I blink.

Is this what Danny looks like when he's giving in?

"You want to dance ... with me?"

He glances at Tim, then Elliot, then finally me. "Why not all of us? We're all here. We're all *friends*. We're all *single*." He lifts his chin. "So let's get out there and ... press our bodies together like a bunch of friendly, horny, *single* men and get ... f-fucking nasty."

I barely have time to form a reply before he grabs me—while Elliot is still attached—and yanks us onto the dance floor. Somewhere behind, Tim follows, asking, "Rome, sir, should I stay in the kitchen? Or should I dance, too? I'm a bad dancer, but I'll try, if you want. Or I could—"

And now it's official: I have no fucking clue where this night is headed.

17. Ride

"WHY DON'T WE GET OUT OF HERE?"

That's the question that changes the whole night.

Was it Elliot who asked it? Tim? Danny? Myself? I don't even remember. The music was too loud. The bodies were too sweaty. The drinks were too drinky. Before I know it, the messed-up quartet of us are stumbling our way out of the elevator. The security guard smirks at us as we pass by. Elliot makes a comment about whether we should ask him to join us, because his muscles were about to bust out of his "adorable uniform". Tim notes how he likes an authoritative guy in uniform, to which Elliot remarks about how quickly he'll get that man *out* of his uniform.

Then we're standing in the street waiting on a cab.

Then we're squished in the back seat of a cab. All four of us. Side-by-side.

I'm in the middle with Elliot, who's half on my lap. Tim is squished on the other side of Elliot like an afterthought, and Danny is on my other side. With my arms over the back of the seat on either side, the slight bulge of my crotch is on

161

full display, which Elliot has taken advantage of, his hand resting on my inner thigh like it's waiting in line.

Danny's eyes are glued to it, every fiber of his being acutely aware of the occupancy of my thighs.

I give him a smirk. "Jealous?"

Danny rolls his eyes and looks away.

It's obvious the sexual frustration is mounting. He's going to burst any second. "I do have *two* thighs, you know. Wanna put your hand on the other?"

"What are you?" asks Danny rather snippily. "A wishbone?"

"You tell me. I've got a bone in my pants, and I've been told I'm good at making wishes come true."

That doesn't earn another response from Danny, who just glares out the window at the street racing by.

Yep, he wants me, and now he's thinking about it.

"When we get to my place," says Elliot, who is clearly riding a high, "you guys won't have to worry about a thing. I've got it all. Booze. Cocktail mixers. Some uppers, if anyone needs them. Everything you want."

"Ball-gag?" asks Tim.

Elliot wrinkles his face. "Um, no."

Tim shrugs. "Then not *everything* I want."

With a fierce rolling of his eyes, Elliot ignores him and faces me. "I don't know why you insisted on bringing the weirdo along."

"Weird is relative," mutters Tim.

"Hey, hey," I cut in, giving Elliot and Danny a rub of the shoulder with my arms over the back of the seat. "Anything goes with us. Weird. Lame. Fucked-up. Hardcore. No one gets talked down to tonight." I glance at Tim. "Unless he's into it. Wanna wear a leash and have us tug you around, Timmy-Doggy?"

Now it's Tim who wrinkles his face. "I'm not into puppy play." Then he hesitates. "At least I think I'm not. Can we try it another night?"

I can't help but notice Danny's silence. I nudge him—which is oddly difficult to do, being squished up against his side. "You're awfully quiet, *friend*. Are you up for whatever's gonna go down at Eric's place when we get there?"

"It's Elliot," Not-Eric corrects me, listening apparently.

Danny glances at the possessive hand still gripping my thigh. Then he lifts two defiant eyes to me. "I am up for *whatever* you're into tonight, *friend*."

He returned the sass I put into that word. He knows what I'm doing. Why is he being so stubborn? "Y'know, we could just call it a night, you and I. Go hang out at my place, pop some popcorn, and—"

"Ugh, fucking *lame*," cuts in Elliot. "On a night like this? We gotta live it up!"

Danny gives me a look. "Hear that? Your idea is lame. I guess we're going to Elliot's to … *live it up*."

"See? Listen to your friend Danny," says Elliot, his grip tightening on my thigh as he rubs it. "Isn't 'live it up' your middle name, Romeo? Or is it Montague? You're such an anti-romantic, I love that you have a name like Romeo."

An anti-romantic? "Huh? What do you mean an—?"

"You've got that much right," says Danny, cutting me off. "If there's anything I've learned tonight, it's that Romeo is always up for a good time. An 'anti-romantic', as you put it."

Is this part of the game? I shrug. "Who needs romance? *Romeo & Juliet* is the most misunderstood play of all time. It isn't about true love, not even close. It's about horny, entitled teenagers defying their families and running off together."

Elliot laughs loudly at that. Too loudly. Right into my ear. "You are so *funny!* I can't get enough of you! 'Horny, entitled teenagers'! Hah!"

His hand rubs my thigh with more vigor. I notice. My dick notices.

Danny notices.

"Just being serious," I go on. "Everyone's standard for romantic expression is a lie."

"Ugh, and he's *smart*, too," sings Elliot.

"It's true," says Tim in a tiny voice. "My idea of romance is him letting me rub his feet in a movie theater. That type of dynamic is a kind of love. At least for me it is. I knew Romeo wasn't into it, but he pretended to be so that I didn't feel weird about my … interests."

Elliot rolls his eyes, then starts rubbing my thigh and eyeing me, like he might not be able to wait until we've arrived at his place to have a taste.

And Danny just now makes the connection. "Wait a sec. You're *that* guy?"

"Who?" asks Elliot, annoyed.

Danny peers across both of us at Tim. Tim lifts his

eyebrows with surprise and says, "Oh, you mean me? Rome told you about me?"

Elliot glances back and forth between us, his thigh rubbing stopped. "Uh, what? Who? Am I missing something here …?"

Danny stares at me hard now. "Who *haven't* you fucked from Denise's party?"

I stare at Danny, struck by his harsh question.

"He didn't fuck me," clarifies Tim in a tiny voice, then adds: "*I'm not really into butt stuff.*"

Elliot raises his hand. "He hasn't fucked me either, but I plan to change that by the end of the night, since I heard from both Antoine *and* Lee that Mr. Romeo here is *legendary* in the bedroom, and it's been a minute since I've had someone take charge and bang me senseless. Apparently you've got this whole bad-boy thing going on? Is that true, Mr. Anti-Romantic Romeo?"

The more Elliot blabs on, the more I feel my plan crumbling to white-hot shreds of dumpster-fire regret in my hands. This seems all wrong suddenly. "Look, I'm not some kind of 'bad boy' who—"

"Seriously, Romeo," he says, his voice low and deep as his hand slides further up my leg and gives it a suggestive squeeze, mere inches from my cock, "I wish I could just make out with you right now, but I have a thing about the back seats of cabs …"

"What's stopping you?" asks Danny rather curtly, picking up every word—and every squeeze of this man's hand on my leg.

"Um … the present company, for one," starts Elliot, adopting a sudden attitude.

"Don't worry about me one bit. I'm sure Romeo here will meet all of your expectations." Danny's body is so tense, I feel like I'm sitting next to an iron-plated wall. "Apparently I don't know my friend as well as I thought. He's got … quite a lot of experience in making people either feel really good— or feel like shit. Isn't that what an anti-romantic 'bad boy' is supposed to do?" He leans forward and taps on the driver's seat. "Excuse me, sir."

The plan is over. Called off. Done. "Danny, I—"

"Please pull over and let me out."

"Danny, wait."

The cab quickly pulls to the curb. Out Danny goes.

"Just let him go," says Elliot as I stare after Danny, shocked. "He seems a bit wound up tight, anyway. We'll probably have more fun without him. *And maybe without your weird friend, too.*"

I give Elliot's words as much attention as a fly in my face. I'm out of the cab in the next instant. "Danny," I call out. "Danny, please, stop." Then I ditch the cab altogether and start going after him. "Danny, where are you going??"

He spins around. His face is stern and red, wearing an expression I've never seen before. "I don't know why you're chasing after me, Romeo. You've got a guy there who is clearly ready to have his way with you. Two, actually. They seem to be at the quicker pace of a relationship you require. Maybe the one can give you a foot rub while you're doing the other. Whatever makes you happy."

"Romeo!" calls out Elliot from the cab. "What're you doing?? This guy can't wait on us forever!"

I ignore all of that and stay with Danny. "None of that makes me happy. You said you wanted to take it slow, didn't you? You're the one who put the brakes on us."

"I might've braked a little, but I didn't expect it to cause you to ... steer into whatever's happening in that cab." Indignation burns in Danny's eyes. "The way you spoke to me in front of them ..."

"Don't lie. You're into that, aren't you? You like it when a guy asserts himself." I come right up to him. "I watched it all the time back when you still worked at Jesse's."

"Huh? What are you talking about?"

"The way Joey used to treat you. The way he was. It taught me all I need to know. Guys like me? The kind of guy I've become?" I bring a gentle hand to Danny's hair. "I'm the kind of guy you want. You don't want the soft 'sweetie' you met a year ago. I know you too well. You get bored of that. You want the new me—the new Romeo."

Danny searches my eyes.

Then he swats my hand away.

I sigh. "Come on, Danny. Give up this stupid hard-to-get game you're playing. I respected your wish to 'take things slow', but I know that's not what you want."

"This is your idea of respecting my wish? By flirting with other guys in front of me and daring to go home with them? By forcing me into a situation where you're ... essentially demanding that we have sex just because you're impatient?"

There's a demonstrative sigh from the cab, where I spot

Elliot throwing his hands. "Fuck this shit," he calls out at us. "You both obviously got something you need to work out. I've lost all interest. Good night, and good luck, you cock-teasing bastard. I'm out." He slides back into the cab, and with a groan of its engine, the vehicle drives away.

I face Danny. "I don't care about Elliot, okay? I never did. I don't care about any of those guys at Denise's party, either."

"Yeah, I heard that much, too," says Danny. "All of the guys whose hearts you broke. One hot night, then toss them aside like they meant nothing to you. I … I didn't think you were like that, Romeo."

"That's because they don't matter to me. I am only here for *you*, Danny. Why else do you think I underwent this transformation over the past year? I needed to see what life was like on the other side."

"The other side??"

"Yeah. The type of guys you like. The Joeys of the world. I wanted to know what it's like to be them. And now I know." I take a step toward him. "Now I'm ready for you, Danny."

"What??" He takes a step back. "This isn't you, Romeo."

The look in his eyes—a mixture of pity and anger—hits me like a sack of bricks over the face. I stop, confused by it. "What do you mean?"

"This … This isn't what I want. Not at all. After Joey, I vowed to never put myself in a situation like that again."

"But you were with him for two years."

"Sure, it was great with him at first. Maybe it was even love. But then he became another person, an angry person, a jealous person … and I just settled for it, accepted it as my fate. When we broke up, only then did I realize the cage I'd locked myself in. I won't go into that cage again, Romeo."

"Danny …"

"Don't you realize this is exactly why Joey and I aren't together anymore? I don't want a guy like that. I'll *never* be with a guy like that again. I don't want …" His eyes swell with tears. "I don't want a jerk. You're … You're both the fucking same now, you and Joey."

His words sting, scuttling across my skin like bitter ice, freezing me.

"The Romeo I knew," he goes on, "he … he would never have acted like this. He wouldn't have taken my heart and tossed it around like a game."

"Danny …"

"He knew how to honor another man. And respect him. And treat him with dignity and loyalty and kindness." He backs away completely from me, shaking his head. "I don't know this Romeo. I don't know you at all."

"Of course you know me." *Is he kidding me right now?*

A tear falls from Danny's eye. He wipes it away instantly, like it was never there. "I'm not a prize to win. I'm not a game, Romeo."

"I know that."

"Do you?" He comes back up to me, bringing his beautiful face close to mine, but nothing about it feels warm or deserved. "Remember what I told you that night long ago? I said you needed to love that man in the mirror before you can expect anyone to give you their heart. I said it and I truly meant it." His eyes drop to my chest. "You need to look into that mirror again."

Something wet touches my hair. Raindrops.

Then more.

Then even more.

In a matter of seconds, the street is filled with the noisy music of a rain shower.

Danny meets my eyes. There is only hurt in them. "No matter how I feel about you, Romeo ... I'm not making this same mistake again."

He turns and walks away.

And for whatever stupid reason, I don't follow him. Does some part of me think he's right? Is that why his words paralyzed me so effectively, I can't fucking move? I just stand here with my own confused heart in my hand, pumping, lonely, lost, as the night sky opens over me in buckets of mockery.

18. Jerk

IT'S IMMEDIATELY AFTER DANNY LEAVES ME ON THE STREET that I hear a voice from behind through the torrent of rain. "Sorry, sir."

I turn around.

Tim stands there.

I'm confused for a second. "Didn't you just leave in the—?"

"Cab? No. Despite Elliot being one of the most beautiful men I've ever met—and so powerful and demanding—I don't think he's into me. He was only there for you. Besides, no ball-gags or leather harnesses at his place? He has a lot to learn if he wants to handle all of *this* someday." He comes up to me. "Are you going to go after him? Your Danny guy?"

I lean against the brick wall of the nearest building, slightly out of the rain. It's cold and rough against my back. "No."

"I'm sorry it didn't work out. I could tell you had feelings for him."

I look at Tim. "Really?"

171

"Of course. It was obvious. Why do you think Elliot was trying so hard? He wanted to pull your focus away from Danny. I can see the appeal, though."

"The appeal?"

"Of a genuine guy like Danny." He shakes his head. "You should've been nicer to him, sir. You should've just been yourself. I know the real you, too. I met him in a movie theater."

I roll my eyes and look away. "That 'me' is dead."

"If you don't mind, I'd like to suggest he isn't. Otherwise you wouldn't still be standing here in the rain, like you're waiting for him to come back. It isn't too late. He's just around the corner."

"If he doesn't want me ..." I can't even finish the sentence. I just drop my gaze to the shiny, wet pavement, and a puddle that pops and crackles like shattered glass from the rainfall. "I don't chase after guys. Not anymore."

Tim leans against the wall next to me. "Too bad." He gazes off down the street. "Danny is a one-of-a-kind fellow. Not my type at all. Too sweet. But definitely a needle in a needlestack."

"That's not the saying." I eye the puzzle that is Tim. "Why don't you think a sweet guy like Danny could give you what you want?" I ask him, annoyed. "If you only go after the jerks, that's all you'll get. People who overlook you. People who treat you mean. People who don't get you."

"But I like being treated that way. It's my thing."

"No. You like a guy to dominate you. That's why you swiped right on my profile pic so long ago. You saw some

172

misleading pic I used—me, sweaty in a gym, looking dominant and full of attitude. That's the experience you craved, the fantasy you built up in your head. Being dominated is understandable. But a nice guy could just as easily *act* mean to you in the bedroom, if you wanted him to, and if you're both into it. Tie you up, tease you, drive you crazy, then after you've had your kinky fun, he'll kiss and cuddle you and actually stick around. A nice guy with your kinks. Maybe even another *Tim* out there, just like you. Don't you want something like that?"

Tim thinks it over. "Hmm. Kinda like you almost did for me at that movie theater?"

I shrug and thrust my hands into my pockets. Honestly, my heart isn't in this conversation. My heart was taken away by the guy who just walked off and left me here in the rain. "Something like that. Anyway, I'm heading home. I don't care how far it is on foot. Night, Tim." I start making my way.

The rain is so loud, I don't even realize Tim is following me until three whole blocks later.

I stop under the awning of a restaurant and face him. "Why are you—?"

"I have a question," he cuts me off, "and I know neither of us will get any sleep tonight unless you answer it."

I sigh. "I don't feel like answering any—"

"This is the question: Does it feel better being the type of guy you used to hate?"

My lips are parted with whatever I was about to say. Now I'm frozen in place with a sudden bonfire of indignation burning inside my chest. A hundred defensive remarks flit past my lips, but none of them come out.

How can one little question destroy a person at once? *The type of guy you used to hate …*

"Tell me why you did it," says Tim, taking a seat at an empty outdoor table, conveniently right there next to us under the awning. "I want to know why you became such a jerk since the last time I saw you. I think it'll help us both to understand better, if you talk me through it."

"I … I don't owe you any explanation," I spit back at him, something deep inside me seething from even being asked such a question. Still, inexplicably, I answer him. "I was sick of being invisible. I wanted guys to look at me. Now guys look at me. What else is there to know?"

"You seem to act as if being a jerk and having a muscular body are the same thing. But they aren't. You can be a jerk and look like me. You can be a nice guy and look like you."

"What's your point?"

"Are you happy?"

Whether it's the relentless rain, his dry yet caring tone of voice, or my own pain, I find all of the fight fleeing my system at once. I have nothing left. No defenses. No explanations. No bitter remarks. Just the noise of the rain, a stinging silence in my heart, and the question still left unanswered.

Are you happy?

I drop into the chair across from him. "No."

"Tell me why you did it."

I lower my gaze to the table. Finally, a gate opens inside

my chest, and it all comes out. "I'm not sure when it was, but there was this ... this *moment* sometime last year when I was in the middle of working out and learning all the ropes ... somewhere between the 'me' I used to be and the 'me' I am now ... and I still noticed and pined for the hotties at the gym, the ones who ignored me. I told myself right then I would never become one of them, not truly. I could change what it means to be a buff hottie. I wouldn't look down on anyone. I'd give attention to the nice guys, the smaller guys, the invisible guys ... I wouldn't ignore them, wouldn't treat them the same shitty way I've been treated my whole life."

"Sounds noble."

"But the more time and effort I put into my workouts and myself ... I started to grow this resentment in my heart for every nice guy I saw. It was like they had become the part of me I hated. When I looked at them, I saw my past. I saw niceness as weakness. I saw what I was running away from with every bicep curl, with every protein shake, with every burning fire in my legs as I did my squats ... with every drop of sweat that ran down my back." My jaw tightens. "And I hated them."

Tim reaches across the table and pats my hand. "That wasn't so hard, was it?"

I wrinkle up my face. "Huh?"

"I bet you feel loads better, too."

"Not really."

"You know what a profile pic actually represents?"

I shrug. "A lie we visually tell in order to get a date who ultimately won't be into us? That's what my best friend

Prisha sorta used to say." I feel a pang of hurt when I realize what I just said. "My … *ex*-best friend, that is."

"Hmm, maybe. Here's another theory." He takes my hand. "It's who we *want* to become. Our friends may mean well, but they tend to hold us back. They want to keep us exactly the way we are, because it's comfortable for them. Family, too. But how else are we supposed to free the spirits of our secret wishes, other than through expression of such things as a different picture of ourselves, or clever words in a dating profile? Maybe the pic I swiped right on isn't so far from a truth that's buried inside you."

"What truth? That I secretly wanted to be a dominant gym-rat asshole?"

"No. That you desired confidence."

I stare at our hands, taken by that thought.

"So the question isn't whether you've become something you hate," says Tim. "You really haven't. You're still you. It's whether, after this rather insane and slightly destructive journey you've apparently taken, you finally have acquired the confidence you always wanted … the confidence you might have unknowingly been admiring in people such as Danny's ex."

I eye him. "You really were listening to everything I was saying, huh?"

"Yes. It's a character flaw, my interest in others." He clears his throat. "I recommend contacting Danny again sometime soon, but not before taking a good look in the mirror—just as he advised. But don't do it with hate or regret. Do it with hope and inspiration. It's sexier, and Danny would like it that way, I truly believe." He lets go of my hand and rises from the table. "If you don't mind, I'm gonna go check out a sex store we passed a few blocks ago. I'm in the mood to wear a ball-gag tonight, even if it's just me alone in my apartment jerking off. What's a single, dateless guy left with anyway, except his hand, his mind, and the freedom to jerk?" Tim gives me a pleasant smile, then turns and disappears into the rain.

I sit at that table awhile, staring at the hand he let go of. Thoughts dance around my mind, torturing me, taunting me. I feel like I've ruined everything. I've gone about all of this wrong. I've thought about all of this wrong. I have made a total, selfish mess out of my life.

And it all started with that kiss I should never have stolen a year ago. A kiss I didn't deserve.

Maybe Joey was right. I had no right to kiss Danny. That was wrong. I see that wholeheartedly now.

Am I feeling sympathy even for Joey? For some shallow, meathead jerk like Joey?

Perhaps that was the point all along.

My mind was just as closed as his.

A sudden buzz in my pocket startles me. I pull out my phone to find a text from my dear partner-in-crime Jonathan asking whether I'm banging Danny yet.

I decide to call him back. "Hey, man. I've got a question for you. Do you ever miss Jonty?"

He sputters like a gasping water faucet before answering. "Say what? Huh? I haven't been called that in … I don't even know how long. Why the hell are you asking that? Is this …

Is this your post-sex euphoria when you get all thoughtful and philosophic?"

"This is me wondering what the hell I've been doing with the last year of my life—and what for." I hug myself as I sit at this empty table, the rain bringing in the cold, too. "I think I miss Rome."

"You've never been to Rome."

"You know what I mean."

He snorts into the phone. "Look, I dunno what's up with you right now, but I'm about to bang the hottest chick I've met in months, and you're … kinda totally killing the mood." He lowers his voice. "And to answer your question, I don't miss that Jonty loser one fucking bit."

I bite my lip and shrug. "It's your right to feel that way. I can respect it."

"Uh … thanks?"

"I just remember that day in the gym, when we first met. I remember the sweet look in your eyes. I wonder if I might have judged you too soon. Maybe it wasn't fear or cowardice that made you relinquish that bicep machine to that other guy. Maybe it was compassion." I bite my lip. "Jonty wasn't a bad guy. He … was rather quite beautiful, in his own way."

There is silence. Then: "What the fuck …?"

"Have fun with your date, buddy. I hope someday you find one you don't have to kick out by morning. You deserve someone like that. I care about you, man."

Then I hang up and peer to the side at the large window of the restaurant next to me. My reflection stares back, hair sopping wet and dripping, eyes curious and faraway.

19. The Mirror

MR. MILTON PACES IN FRONT OF THE ROOM, HIS FINGERS twitching irritably as they grip his mug of coffee. He takes one slurp of it after asking all of us his latest million-dollar question.

The question being: "Who do I need to fire?"

This is coming after a recent report that our all-new "getting some" marketing angle isn't testing well. The fitness company that hired us doesn't like any of it. The test groups are mixed at best, either being repulsed or amused for the wrong reasons. No one is happy.

Least of all Mr. Milton, who continues to pace the front of the room, and asks us yet again: "Who do I need to fire?"

It's been about a week since the party I went to with Danny when I ruined everything. I've spent a lot of time in my own head. My phone's been on silent. I haven't spent a single night out with Jonathan. No dates. No texts. Ignoring every ding of my dating app.

Just me, myself, and I.

And it sucks.

Especially now, sitting in this room, while my boss continues to interrogate us. My eyes keep finding Prisha across the table from me, who hasn't looked at me once since the day I tore her down in this very room. I felt a stab of pride that day.

And now when I think about it, all I feel is shame.

Who am I becoming?

She's toying with a pen in her hand, her notebook opened in front of her, full of notes and ideas and brilliance. Everyone else in the room is anxiously picking at their fingers, or gnawing on their lips, or otherwise desperately not wanting to be seated at this table, made to answer for our abysmal work.

And on and on Mr. Milton drones, with his same stupid question no one dares to answer. "Who do I need to—?"

"Me, I guess."

Everyone turns their faces, startled by my sudden answer.

Mr. Milton as well, who quirks an eyebrow my way. "Excuse me?"

I shrug. "You keep asking the question. I gave you an answer. The whole idea came from something I didn't even mean to suggest when I insulted your penis. Or was it your sex life? The marketing campaign is a failure before it's even left the ground, and that's all because of one very simple reason." I spread my hands. "It sucked."

Mr. Milton's eyes are stony and blank. He says nothing.

I glance at my tablemates. "Why were you all so hard for my idea, anyway? Were you just caught up in the moment of me making fun of our boss? Talking back to the douchebag

180

who's given us a thankless hell of an environment to work in for the past few years? Honestly, my idea *was* juvenile, and there was only one person at this table with balls enough to say it." I peer across the table at Prisha.

She meets my stare with surprise.

"Prisha had the better idea," I go on. "She had the smarter angle. People love fads. People like to follow trends. Make being fit a fad. Make being fit a trend. The demographic we're targeting don't trust the 'gorgeous and sexy' to make decisions for them anymore. They're smarter than that. They want to own their own health, their own standards of beauty, their own bad-assery." I smirk. "Sounds to me like Prisha was on to something golden, something we should've listened to."

Prisha squints suspiciously at me.

I peer at Mr. Milton, who has stopped pacing to frown at me. "So I guess the answer to your pressing question is: you should fire me. If not for providing the bad idea, then for talking to you in the manner that I did then—and am now. Regardless of how poorly you treat us, I shouldn't return the behavior. As you once pointed out to me, you're the only one who gets paid for your attitude."

A frigid silence passes in which no one seems brave enough to say a word, let alone even breathe. Juan looks like he shit a brick in his chair. Prisha seems pensive and uncertain. Mr. Milton has changed the expression about twelve times on his face, now settling on a sort of pursed-lip look, like he's sucking on something bitter.

Finally, he tilts his head. "You really think I treat you so poorly?" Then he sighs. "Never mind. You're not fired. I'm too lazy to do any paperwork today, let alone lose the only voice in the room willing to speak up to me. Go on, then, Prisha," he says with a gesture of his mug at her. She turns to him, eyes wide. "Take the floor. Present us with your ideas. I know that notebook in front of you is filled with them."

Prisha, after one last glance at me, clears her throat and wastes no time. I smile inwardly as she shares her brilliance with the room.

For the first time in a year, I feel like I'm taking a step in the right direction.

The challenge is to keep *stepping in the right direction.*

It seems like a blink of an eye later when I'm slipping onto the elevator, my day of work done. Quite frankly, I'm ready for another night of retrospection and tea-sipping. As it turns out, I've developed a taste for hot tea over the past week. Imagine that.

Prisha slips in after me. "What was that about?" she asks.

The elevator doors close. We slowly descend. "What was *what* about?" I ask coyly.

"You basically cut off your figurative balls in front of everyone, I hope you know."

"Yes, I know."

She smirks at me. "And still he didn't fire you."

"I'm basically a cockroach." I half-turn to her, all the humor leaving my tone. "It was the right thing to do, Prisha."

She doesn't respond to that, but her eyes remain on the side of my face. I feel that same softness in her that I felt the last time we shared an elevator ride, like she's looking for the old me.

Maybe it's more visible this time.

We arrive at the first floor, and as I step off the elevator, she stops me with, "You want to grab a smoothie before heading home?"

I give her a surprised look. "You aren't going into Jesse's Fitness today?"

She rolls her eyes. "You mean uselessly walking on a treadmill for an hour? I'll get enough exercise walking to our favorite smoothie joint." She hesitates. "Assuming it's still your favorite."

I smile. "Of course it is."

She smiles back.

It's a strange feeling, talking to her again. It's like not a single day has passed since the last time we chatted so openly. Yet everything is different. I'm not the same person I was. And despite the snide remark I made to myself about Prisha not changing in the least, it's obvious she actually *has* done a lot of growing of her own this past year.

I find myself very interested to hear all about it.

The moment we're out of the building, we're confronted by a frantic face: Jonathan's. "Dude, I've been calling you every day. Why the hell aren't you answering my texts? I swear, you cast some kind of spell on me last week when you asked if I missed 'Jonty'. I've been messed up in the head. I couldn't go through with that woman that night. Something felt off. Something felt missing. Something felt ..."

He draws silent the moment his eyes lock onto Prisha, stunned by the sudden awareness of her existence. Whatever was in Jonathan's angry eyes is gone.

"I, uh …" He lowers his voice. "S-Sorry. I got a little carried away. Or something. Hi." He extends a hand, then suddenly drops it. "Sorry, that was weird. Are you a friend of, uh, Romeo's …? I'm Jonty." His eyes flash when he realizes he used his old nickname. "Sorry. I meant Jonathan."

She gives him a look that can best be described as a visual representation of WTF. "Prisha."

"Prisha. What a … a beautiful name." He leans into me at once. *"Who's this babe??"*

I eye him. "My friend and coworker, and we're grabbing smoothies together." I give him a pat on the shoulder. "Sorry for the radio silence. I'm just going through a thing. But for now, a drink with my friend Prisha is in order. I'll call you later, buddy."

As I walk off with Prisha, she glances over her shoulder at him. Jonathan is watching us walk away, as if the cartoon version of himself still hasn't picked his jaw up off the pavement. She smirks and calls out at him, "I like 'Jonty' better. Suits you."

I have no idea what Jonathan does with that piece of information, because soon Prisha and I round the corner, and off we go.

It isn't much longer before the two of us are sitting by a window, sipping our respective smoothies. Strawberry banana for me, ginger plum for her. Only small talk has been tossed back and forth so far over this tiny table separating us.

Then comes the good stuff. "What went wrong, Rome?"

I'm stirring my smoothie with the thick straw, pondering. "I ask myself that all the time. What was I doing wrong? Why

184

couldn't I find a guy for me? I decided I needed a change. I would 'learn from the greats'. That is: all the assholes I dated previously who made me feel weak. I decided I would never again feel weak. I took control of my life. I decided: *I* was the only one who could choose how other guys made me feel. Was it really any of my exes who hurt me? Or was it myself, for being so 'nice', for putting myself in those situations? Nice isn't good, I decided. Nice is the naïve thing you do to make others comfortable. It means nothing. 'Nice' is as great a lie as cheating." I consider my remaining smoothie, thinking on all the men that passed through my bed. "Maybe that's what makes the bad guy good: the way he approaches the dating world with honesty. I decided I'd never lie to myself again. I'd never lie to others with another 'nice' act. The nice guy in me was dead."

When I meet Prisha's eyes, I don't find them impressed or moved.

In fact, she looks frozen mid-eye-roll when she asks: "Are you done?"

I frown. "You asked what went wrong."

"I didn't want to interrupt your little dramatic soliloquy there, *Romeo*, but you aren't talking about the guy you did all of this for. That's what I was really asking about." She pushes her smoothie aside and folds her arms on the table, getting to business. "Danny. The guy who took your heart. The *real* reason you went through all of this."

I don't think I've heard his name out loud since the last time I saw him. It makes my heart jump. I drop my gaze to the table, emotions flooding into me. "I guess I ... got caught up this whole past year chasing some version of myself I don't think I was meant to be. I got lost along the way, chasing the heart of a guy I don't deserve."

"What makes you think you don't deserve him?"

"Do you really need to ask?"

Prisha sighs. "Okay, Rome. Listen to me. And I want you to *really* listen to me. Don't do that pretend thing you do where you just hear what you want to hear."

I frown at her. "I hate that you know me so well, even still."

"Some things never change." She leans forward. "You're a good person. You've made mistakes. But even the best people make mistakes. They fall down. They do terrible things. But the difference between them and the *real* jerks of the world is that they know the difference. They feel guilt and shame. They want to do better. I see the fight in your eyes, Rome. You aren't ready to give up on this Danny guy, and you won't."

"I don't know. I feel like it's beyond repair, my relationship with Danny, if I can even dignify it with the word 'relationship'."

"Nothing is beyond repair."

"So what do I do?"

"It's simple." A soft smile touches her lips. "Be your sweet self. Unapologetically. Work on being the truest version of you, with no expectations and no judgment. This isn't a ploy, Rome, nor is it a game. It isn't a scheme to win your guy back. Just patiently work on yourself first. You must be willing to face the mirror and see yourself not only for what you really are, but for the kind of person you are capable of becoming. And let me tell you from experience, there is nothing sexier than honesty."

I find myself taking hold of her hand across the table. Prisha's smile grows. I feel like I have my friend back.

"And for the love of God," she adds, "delete that fucking dating app. I don't suspect you will be needing it anymore."

It's those words that circle my head that same evening when I'm back home and my phone is out of my pocket, resting in my palm, facing me like an old foe. I tap the screen and stare my dating app in the face. I press a finger on the icon until the delete button appears.

I stare at its cold, red, X-shaped face for too long, weighing all of the imaginary pros and cons. Even with the list of cons being overwhelming and long, I actually still debate keeping the app.

It calls out to me. An easy option.

A siren's song.

Stay and be miserable with me, it seems to sing.

So many viable options to consider, it reminds me, flirting with me in the voices of a dozen horny, fake-interested men.

You'll never be alone again, it promises, begging me not to press that cold red X.

One flash of Danny's sweet face destroys all of that noise. I proudly jab my thumb on that X, like I'm spearing a monster straight through its heart. I watch with bittersweet victory as the app vanishes from the screen of my phone, its data deleted, gone.

20. Perfectly

SUDDENLY, TEA IS MY NEW THING.

Prisha joins me sometimes. And other days, I go by myself. The atmosphere is perfect and calming, which is exactly what I didn't realize I needed. If I'm not conversing with Prisha, I'm in a world of my own looking out the big front windows where I meet the eyes of people walking by, similarly lost in their own thoughts. I feel connected to each and every one who passes, and yet so far away from anything or anyone I know.

The funny thing is, it takes half a week of sitting here at this window before I realize what's across the street from me.

A vitamin and nutritional supplements store.

It couldn't be the same one, could it?

Then the doors open, as if cued to do so at this exact moment, and Danny appears.

What a sight. Danny's in a tight white uniform polo and khakis with a stylish belt. He seems to have been sent out to clean the display windows, spray bottle and rag in hand. I watch him for a moment, a smile touching my lips.

He stops wiping the windows, as if something just occurred to him. Then he turns and, for no seeming reason, looks my way.

I glance down at my tea, as if contemplating it. Then I lift it to my lips for a sip and gaze away.

Does he see me through the window? Is he watching me right now?

Finally, I dare to glance his way.

He's looking right at me.

A moment passes where neither of us seem to move. A rag and bottle of cleaner hang from his hands. A cup of tea rests in mine. Is he waiting for me to acknowledge him first, or am I?

He looks away, then faces the window again and resumes cleaning. Moment's over. I nod to myself with understanding, then resume making love to my tea.

The next time I see Danny is at our gym. It catches me by surprise, since I haven't seen him here since that night. I'm doing bicep curls when I notice Danny a few benches over doing his own. I can't be sure if he knows I'm here too, but I have to assume he does.

Someone eclipses my view of the mirror—some guy I've never met with a buzzed head, muscles everywhere, and a suggestive smirk. "Hey there," he greets me. "Need a spot, hot shot?"

That's three rhyming words in a row. I wonder how many times he rehearsed that line.

"Nope," I answer. "I'm good all on my own, thanks."

The guy quirks an eyebrow. "You sure?"

"Totally."

After a dubious look at me, he finally leaves me alone, and I resume my set. After I finish and rest my arms, I notice Danny glancing my way. Of course the moment I turn to him, he looks away, then quite suddenly decides to relocate to a machine somewhere else.

But I'm pretty sure he witnessed the exchange.

Then in the locker room later, I get to enjoy a lovely berating from Jonathan. "Again??" he cries out as we're changing. "Dude, you haven't had a night out with me in weeks. What's up with you? I'm having to do the whole routine myself, and it's boring, and … Romeo, are you even listening?"

"Maybe I'm just not into it anymore," I say as I shrug on my shirt.

Jonathan sighs as he leans against the locker. "So level with me. What's going on? What aren't you telling me? Why aren't we getting ass every night anymore?"

I face him. "Maybe a year ago, we had something to prove. To the assholes who stole the attention. To the dating world we kept stumbling through. But what about to the person who really matters?—to ourselves? Haven't we proven enough?"

Jonathan scrunches up his face, confused.

"I gotta get home," I tell him as I sling my backpack over a shoulder. "Give myself some self-love with a nice book and maybe some hot tea. It's my new routine. You should try it."

With Jonathan still staring at me like I just turned into a banana, I turn to make my way to the door, only to be stopped by the sight of Danny at a nearby locker. I'm guessing he heard everything, because there's a curious glint in his eyes as he gazes at me, lost in thought.

I give him a tiny wave.

He gives me a subtle nod back.

Nope, we still don't talk.

But the next day, we do.

He approaches me after I finish a set on the leg press machine. "Hey," he greets me, hands in the pockets of his gym shorts.

I gaze up at him from the bench. "Hi, Danny."

He seems unsure what to say. "You ... seem to be doing well."

"Thanks, Danny. I appreciate it."

He nods, then looks away.

I decide he's fishing, and I bite. "I've been taking a lot of time to work on myself lately. Someone wise told me I have to love myself before expecting to give my heart away."

Danny tries not to smile. His eyes meet mine, soft and sweet. "Sounds like whoever said that might have only had your best interest in mind."

I nod in agreement. "I believe they did."

"Well ... I don't want to interrupt your workout." He nods at me. "Good to see you again, Romeo." Then he walks away, and I watch him, a little warmth returned to my heart.

Is that his way of nudging our door back open?

I'm certain that's the closest thing I'll get to a cue from Danny.

The next time I'm in the area for tea, I decide to head

across the street instead. The nutrition shop is brightly lit and surprisingly colorful inside. Several scents hang in the air, from garlic, to peppermint, to something oaky and woodsy. I survey the aisles of the store, glancing at each of the supplements on the shelves. I expect most vitamin and supplement shops to be sterile, cold, and medicinal. This place is full of color and life—much like the special person I'm here to see.

Then I round the corner, and I see him. Danny, restocking a shelf.

He glances my way, then stops.

I stop as well, a smile on my face.

That's when some random coworker of his steps right in front of me, blocking my view. "Can I help you find something, sir?" he asks sweetly.

I keep my eyes on Danny as I answer the guy. "I'm wondering if you might have any supplements that can help me."

"Of course, sir. What do you need?"

"I need something for a broken heart."

Danny smirks.

The guy sputters. "I-I … uh …"

"I also need something for a wounded, overinflating ego," I add, still watching Danny. "Something to curb my odd tendency lately of being mean. I've been a bad friend, a bad date, and a bad human being."

The guy clears his throat. "I'm not sure we have anything that—"

Danny cuts in. "Or maybe you can just … ask me nicely

to try again."

The guy steps aside, surprised, then belatedly realizes Danny and I have been having a sort of secret conversation over his head.

I come forward. "Try again?"

"Sure." Danny approaches me, too. "Let's have dinner. I think I'd like that. An honest, respectable dinner with an honest, respectable man."

We're in front of each other now. "Are you sure I'm either of those things?"

"I've seen what I've seen of you lately," reasons Danny, "so all I can do is cross my fingers and hope for the best."

"Sounds like a better strategy for a craps table."

"Probably is."

I'm right in front of him. I realize the people at the counter have stopped chatting. Someone else has poked his head out from between the aisles. We have a little audience. I wonder how many of them know exactly who I am, if Danny's told them, if they've been his support system.

"But," he goes on, "I have a suspicion my chances might be better with you."

"You sure about that?"

"Nope."

He still smells the same—clean and inviting, like a precious home I want to live in forever. His eyes are two pools of ageless memories and hope that I'm desperate to dive back into. The soft, subtle way his lips always appear to be on the edge of cracking a smile—that's the essence of Danny that steals my heart. There is something so sweet yet strong about him, something I don't think I'll ever find adequate words for.

So I ask the question. "Do you want to get some dinner with me tonight, Danny Chen?"

Danny seems to weigh the question as he gazes into my eyes. He has such a beautiful way of holding me hostage, like he knows each and every one of my thoughts, my doubts, and my desperate hopes.

Then Danny smiles. "Sure."

My lungs fill with my next breath at last, tasting sweet, sweet relief. "Yeah? You will?"

"Where shall we meet?"

"How about your favorite dim sum place? Seven?"

"Sounds perfect." He nods at me. "See you there ... Romeo."

With that, he slips away, returning to his task of stocking a shelf. I glance to the side, and the people at the counter quickly turn away, resuming their business. I realize after a while that I'm just standing there in a daze. Maybe a part of me didn't think he'd actually give me another shot.

Am I the luckiest motherfucker in this whole city?

"Yes," answers Jonathan an hour later when I'm home. He fidgets near my closet door as I bury myself in it in search of an outfit after my shower. "You are definitely lucky to get another shot, and I'm happy for you, but you still haven't told me enough about Prisha. Is she single? Is she into art? Is she, like, a Level 9 Clinger and I should avoid her at all costs?"

I pull another shirt from the closet, then fling it away with dejection. I just had a shower, I have nothing but a towel around my waist, and I'm a total wreck. What the hell do I wear? "Truth is, Jonty, I think she's way out of your league, far too serious for you, and you should help me find an outfit in this messy closet before I lose my mind."

"Too serious? What do you mean by that?"

"Is this overdressing too much?" I slap a nice shirt to my chest and look in the mirror. Then I swap it out for a shirt and tie combo. "Maybe I *should* overdress. Y'know, to give a good impression."

"Do you think I'm …?" Jonathan leans against the wall, all the steam fleeing his system. "You think I'm not good enough for your friend? Is that it?"

"She is a one of a kind. She is special in so many ways. She is smart. She is driven. She is not just a fun time. Does that sound like the kind of woman you go for?"

"Well, no, but I—"

"Prisha is the *real deal*, Jonty, and—"

"Quit calling me that!"

"Hey, Prisha likes it better," I remind him, "so you should probably get used to it." Then I consider the more casual t-shirt again, holding it up to me with a frown.

Jonathan sits on the bed with a huff. Then he flops onto his back and stares at the ceiling in misery. "Maybe I want a one-of-a-kind lady in my life. Someone special, smart, and driven. Someone …" He grabs his head. "What the hell am I talking about? I'm losing my mind here!"

"Actually, yes, I *will* do a shirt and tie. Danny will appreciate the effort." I smile, then whip off my towel and toss it at the bed.

The towel lands on Jonathan's face. He doesn't even budge. "I can't stop thinking about her!" he moans from underneath the towel, muffled.

"I should feel a protective instinct when it comes to Prisha," I say as I button up my shirt, "but she's a woman who can take care of herself. So if you want to try it, be my guest, but don't be surprised when she turns you down hard and breaks your heart."

He sits up at once, the towel flinging right off of him. "Breaks *my* heart?"

I pull on my pants, tuck in my shirt, then walk up to Jonathan as I do my belt. "If you want to prove you're worthy of Prisha, you have to be willing to put yourself second for once."

"Second ...?"

"Yeah. Y'know." I turn to face the mirror as I adjust my tie. "The exact opposite of what we've been doing this past year."

"I don't understand."

"What I mean is ..." I finish with my tie, do my cuffs, then smirk at myself in the mirror. "... Rome is making a comeback. Maybe it's time Jonty does the same."

Jonathan is still staring at me, baffled, when I go into the bathroom to do my hair and finish getting pretty. He doesn't say anything else. When I emerge to get his approval, he only looks up at me with this strange, faraway look in his eyes.

For a moment, I see Jonty in them. Lost. Confused. Vulnerable. Curious. Quiet.

"Do I look good?" I ask him.

And it's with that same "Jonty" glint in his eyes that he peers at me thoughtfully and says, "I think I need to make amends with my big brother. I'm going to call him. Tonight, actually, right when I get home." He smiles. "And yes, you look good. You look ready."

I smile, proud of my friend. *And I sure as fuck hope I'm as ready as you think, buddy.*

Jonty and I head out together. When we pop out of the door to my apartment building, we stop short on the stoop.

Danny is standing there, leaning against a nearby streetlamp. He's dressed in a sexy, fitted button-down shirt over a pair of slim jeans, with a pop of color for his shoes. His hair is styled adorably, and his eyes sparkle as he gazes up at the sky. When he sees me, his eyes light up and a smile spills over his face.

Jonty gives me a knowing look, says, "Good luck, buddy," then heads off, hands in his pockets, with a pensive expression, likely thinking over his own troubling dilemma.

But that's the last thing on my mind, now that Danny is in front of me. "I thought we were—?"

"Wow," says Danny, taking me in from head to toe. "You sure know how to clean up."

I come up to him. "Weren't we meeting at the restaurant?"

"We were," he says to my chest. "But I thought you could maybe use some company." He meets my eyes. "Maybe we should've gotten a reservation at a fancy restaurant, considering—"

"Oh, you think I'm overdressed?" I come closer to him.

"This isn't a reflection of where we're going. This is a reflection of how I feel about you. The effort I think a person like you deserves."

Danny lifts an eyebrow. "That so?"

"You've seen me at my worst. You've seen me at my weakest. You deserve to see me at my best. I want to be the man of your dreams, Danny, and ... and I'm ready to do whatever it takes to become that. *Whatever* it takes."

He gazes into my eyes, taking all of that in.

Then he squints at me. "Well, maybe we should just start with dinner first ...?"

Okay, maybe I'm being a bit overdramatic. "Dinner first," I agree, laughing self-consciously.

As we make the walk, I can't help but feel giddy, like a high school teenager walking with his prom date to the dance. Now and then, our hands graze, or our shoulders bump on the busier streets. My heart races with every step. It is amazing how much power Danny has over me. He has a way of peeling down my walls with such expertise and compassion, it makes me question why I had any walls up at all. He makes me feel the most "me", no matter what version of that he happens to encounter.

Even if it's the version of me who keeps gnawing on his lip. And checking his breath every five seconds. And stealing nervous glances at the cute guy he's walking next to.

To tell you the truth, it's exhilarating.

That overwhelmingly excited feeling lasts the whole walk to the restaurant, and through the whole dinner. We share a whole damned table of delicious dim sum, ordering nearly half the menu. Someone at the restaurant must be taken by us, because we're brought out two bonus dishes courtesy of the chef, who also comes out to ensure we're happy. After he leaves us to enjoy the rest of our meal, Danny gives me a look and says, "It's definitely your tie," to which the both of us laugh. Every bite is like holding a seasoned, flavorful piece of paradise on our tongues. Every dish smells twice as enticing and delicious as the last. And every time I catch Danny's eyes across the table, neither of us can resist smiling.

This just might be the best night of my life.

When we leave the restaurant, our walk is slower and calmer, chatting casually about all sorts of random things, from my change of pace at work, to antics at his nutrition shop. I've loosened my tie and rolled up my sleeves. It feels like we're our old selves again, maybe even from a year ago when he was unavailable and I was awkward and insecure.

Is this what being happy feels like?

Is it way too soon to tell?

We stop at the crosswalk where our paths diverge. My place is one way. His, the other. As we peer into each other's eyes, I feel like our bodies have become powerful magnets, and it's taking every bit of strength I have not to crash my mouth into his and lose all restraint.

"Well, I guess this is when we call it a night," says Danny.

I nod slowly, understanding. I want to show him I'm a better man. I want to show him my maturity. "I guess it is," I agree. "Only if you're ready to head home."

He shuffles his feet. "If I'm being honest, I … don't want

this night to end."

"Me neither."

"But it … probably should." He bites his lip.

This is the new Romeo, the one who doesn't push, the one who gives his special man the space to breathe, the one who knows self-control—*even if it fucking kills him.* "Don't worry, Danny. This is just one date. We will always have next time."

"Next time?"

"And the time after that, and after that, and after that …" I take hold of his hand suddenly, which startles him. Our eyes move to our fingers as they gently weave together. "There's no rush. I'm not going anywhere. We can have ten more dinners before we do anything else, if that's what it takes."

He peers into my eyes.

I peer into his. "I can wait for you. As long as it takes."

He swallows hard. I feel the tension of *need* rippling through his body like an electric current. "I …"

"Yeah?"

His grip on my fingers tightens. "I … don't think I can wait."

I lift an eyebrow. *Does he mean—?*

The next instant, he pulls me against his body and presses his lips to mine.

And now it's Danny who can't hold back as he clutches me against him, kissing me like this may be the last time he ever kisses anyone again. I kiss him right back, feeling as if I've finally reached the other side of this rickety, terrible bridge I've been crossing since I can remember.

Danny is my safe place. He's my destination.

He's my *everything*.

When we pull apart, it feels like the chemistry building between us never stopped. Whatever we had, it's back tenfold, and there's nothing in the way to stop us but ourselves.

"You've never seen my place," Danny points out suddenly.

I can't keep my eyes off of him. "That's true."

"We should fix that."

"Only if you're ready."

He pulls our hips together and gives me a look. "Do I look ready to you?"

Then he kisses me again.

I kiss him right back.

Whatever we've just started, it's a raging firestorm, and it is eager to consume everything in its path—mad, glorious, and unstoppable as it is.

I can't tell you how we get down the street. I can't describe the front of his apartment complex. I can't even tell you which floor he's on or what his apartment number is.

All I know is, Danny won't stop kissing me.

And I can't stop kissing him.

Whatever we've been denying ourselves all this time is at last making itself known. My hands are all over his body and his lips are all over mine as we stumble through his dark apartment, kicking into things on our way to his bedroom— wherever the hell that is. My tie is whipped off in seconds. His shirt, too. Then his fingers fumble blindly for the buttons of my shirt, and it's gone just as fast. My shoes and pants are an afterthought as they're peeled off and flung aside. When my back hits the bed, he's on top of me in an instant, claiming me like a prize.

Then our fire calms as we gaze into each other's eyes, as if startled by what we've just kindled together. More slowly, he presses his lips to my neck, then to my chest, where he cherishes me like some precious thing. I run my hands up and down his soft back, savoring every moment, taking my time.

His wet tongue drags over my nipple, where he starts to get especially playful and teasing.

I squirm, then let out a happy sigh.

His hand slides up the side of my body, then my neck, and across my cheek, where his fingers tangle themselves in my hair. As he runs his hand through it, I can't help but be reminded of a night when that very action drove me wild. I think he must be reminded of it, too, because he looks up at me and smiles with a playful twinkle in his eye.

Something comes over me. "Danny, we don't have to do anything, if you don't want to," I tell him. "We can just hang out. We can just chill, take the night to relax, or—"

"I don't want to chill. I don't want to relax." He rises from my chest and climbs back up to my face, as if to get a better look at me through the darkness. "I just want you."

"I want you, too, but ..." I let out a sudden chuckle. "I just want to be sure. You obviously weren't expecting me, since I don't see a 'mood-setter lamp' left on, or—"

"Well, well, someone's learned from a master," he teases. "But you're not just some date I was hoping to take home and impress."

"I'm not?"

"No." He meets my eyes. "You're more."

I part my lips, unsure what to make of that.

When he kisses me again, I forget everything. We roll over on the bed, and it's now me who straddles him as our kissing intensifies. I explore his body with my lips now, and with each kiss to his skin, I show him how much I revere him. He's a treasure who deserves to be coveted. I feel his hands in my hair as I work my way down to his beautiful, perfect cock, which throbs and flexes in its urgency. Each time my lips touch him, I fall deeper and deeper under his spell.

I have imagined time and time again what this moment might feel like. Nothing can possibly have hoped to compare to the real thing. Being intimate with Danny. Tasting his skin. Feeling his warmth against my face.

It's like fucking poetry when I run my tongue up the soft, smooth and supple flesh of his cock, and he moans out with surprise. I reach the firm reddened tip, then lick my way right back down, stroking him in slow motion with my tongue. I can't help but to relish every single second we have tonight.

It's making him lose his mind.

Fuck, I love this too much.

My mouth opens. I let in the tip, close my lips, then tease his firm, mushroom head with my tongue. It must drive him crazy, that agonizingly subtle stimulation of just the head of his cock—not quite enough, and yet far too much. He squirms against me as his fingers curl in my hair, desperate for me to take the rest of him.

And after far too long spent worshipping the tip, when I do finally open my mouth and swallow another inch of him, his sighs become vocal. Danny can't contain himself a second longer. Neither can I. My mouth descends further, taking him all in, all the way down to the base. His cock fills my mouth and inches down my throat as I suck him deeply.

No amount of restraint can possibly hope to contain our appetites now. We've waited far too long to taste each other. We've had too many dreams. Too many lonely nights. Too many wasted hours spent wondering what it would feel like to finally be alone in one another's arms. Even our clothes were a wall between us.

Not anymore.

I lift my mouth off of his cock, give it a few more teasing licks across the head like my favorite lollipop, then eye him. "Has anyone told you that you have the most beautiful dick? It's the perfect size, the perfect shape ..."

"I want you ... in ..."

I lift an eyebrow. "What was that?" Then I crawl back up, bringing my face to his. "You want me ... how?"

He stares at me, out of breath. Then he takes hold of my face suddenly, paves a path of hungry kisses to my ear, where he takes the cutest nip and whispers, "I want you ... inside of me, Rome."

Those just became my favorite words. "You do?"

"Please. I can't stand another second of foreplay. I want you inside of me."

I can barely contain my smile of delight. "*That*, I can do."

"Nightstand, bottom drawer, behind my socks."

That's where I find his lube and condoms. I waste no time peeling off the wrapper, rolling it on, then lubing up. As I climb over Danny again, I hook his toned, shapely legs over my shoulders, then position myself right at his hole, which I tease with a few lubricated fingertips. I have the pleasure of watching Danny's face squirm as I gently torture his hole. He looks like he hasn't had sex in ages, every inch of his body desperate for relief. Even as I massage his hole into a state of total relaxation, his eyes on mine, he licks his fingers and starts stroking himself, resuming right where I'd left off.

The way he looks at me now, with such openness and vulnerability, is something I will do everything in my power to never take advantage of. Danny is a person I don't ever want to hurt again. I will protect him with everything I have. There's no doubt in my mind that he's the most beautiful soul I have ever met, and he deserves any happiness he wants.

And I need to tell him that. "Danny, I promise you, I'll never again—"

"I want you to wreck me," he moans.

I blink. "What?"

"Wreck me. Destroy me. I'm all yours tonight, Rome, every part of me."

Wow. This isn't what I expected in-the-bed Danny to be like. *Not that I'm complaining.* "Are you totally sure? We can still take this slow. I don't want you to feel pressured into anything. You're the one in charge. You've always been."

For a moment, the animal inside him is tamed. He peers at me, floating in the pleasurable space of whatever my fingers are doing to his hole, of how deeply he feels every stroke of his cock, of whatever he anticipates is about to happen when I enter him. I see him hearing my words. I see the joy in his eyes.

His voice softens. "I know you respect me. I know you always did, even when you didn't know how to show it. I've felt nothing but respected and cared for this whole evening."

Yes, we're having this conversation with my lubricated fingertips in his asshole. "I'm glad you see that, Danny. I just want you to know it isn't for show. I truly mean every word."

"I know." He grips the back of my head with his free hand, pulls me in for a kiss, then whispers to my face: "And I mean it when I say I want you to wreck me."

Dear god. "You do?"

"Make me yours. Make me *all* yours. I want you to fuck me so hard, I forget everyone I've ever had sex with before. Fuck me so hard, *you* forget everyone you ever put on a bed, or sent out a door. Because none of them matter. There's only you and me ... and whatever's about to happen."

I can't tell whether that is the most messed-up thing a guy has ever said to me, or the most romantic.

I'm hard as a rock, my heart gallops for him, and my soul is on fire. Of course I can give him exactly what he wants. But no matter how rough I am, or how deeply I pound him, the truth will remain the same: I'm actually all his, and every thought of every guy I've ever known is already long gone.

Danny Chen is the only man who will ever matter.

In fact, I think ... "I think you're the only guy who's ever mattered to me, since the day I met you."

I see his face melt under those words, like I just uttered a secret password that unlocked his heart. "Oh, Romeo ... Romeo, Romeo, Romeo ..."

Well, I should probably get started here before he starts reciting Shakespeare. "Strap in, Danny. I'm about to give you exactly what you want."

My fingers are replaced by my cock.

Danny lets out one small gasp. His eyes rock back.

And I slide inside.

"*Romeo* ..." He moans as I pump him deeply, pinning him to the bed.

I can barely make words. I'm on a whole other plane of existence with Danny in my grip, our bodies connected, our pleasure matching a frequency of its own. "I'm all yours," I breathe in his ear as I go deeper and deeper with every thrust of my hips. I hear our flesh smacking together. I hear his moans and feel the vibrations they make in his chest. Our breaths crash against each other's faces. "I'm all yours," he moans right back. "Wreck me, Romeo, *fuck*, wreck me ..."

There is no amount of casual sex that can replace the real thing. When you are with the man who matters, the man who can steal your heart away with just a glance of his beautiful eyes, you realize how starved you've been all your life. Have you ever actually *had* sex before? Was it all just a joke? Was it all just practice? Why didn't I notice how numb and fruitless all of my past relationships have been?

How could I not have known what I was missing, all this time?

Simply nothing can describe how I feel right now.

We reach our climaxes at the same time. And I can attest

to the fact that that is *rare*. As Danny reaches his point of no return, I watch that distinct, exquisite look of anguish and pleasure twist his face. Then he lets out a groan as he erupts all over his chest and abs. Just from that look on his face alone, I fly right over the edge, emptying myself inside him one desperate, urgent pump at a time. The room fills with our sounds of relief at long last.

Then we draw silent and collapse, my body on his, and our deep breaths in our ears. Neither of us can seem to form a word for quite some time as we swim together in a pool of our afterglow.

"You really did it," he murmurs.

I lift my face to look at his. "Did what?"

"Wrecked me." He turns to look at me. "I'm in pieces. Fallen apart. Destroyed forever." He smiles. "And all yours. I don't think I'll ever be the same after tonight."

I let on an exhausted smile, kiss him, then say, "I guess that makes two of us."

As we lie here on this bed, swirling in a dreamy state of unmatched joy, I'm struck by a sudden thought: This is the first time I can remember having sex and not wanting to leave right away. In fact, I can't imagine leaving at all. I want to stay right here, clinging to Danny, holding him in my arms, and letting the rest of the world fade away.

I have never felt more alive, more complete, more *myself* than I do right now. *Danny, I'm the luckiest man in the world to have gotten a second chance with you.*

Another Year Later

Epilogue

"YOU OWE ME $1500!" SHOUTS JONTY.

"No, no. You only have *one* hotel, not two," says Danny, trying not to get too heated. "And if you had *two*, then—"

"Look, I *let* you be the dog tonight, okay? I have to be the stupid thimble."

"So? Your head looks like a thimble."

"Dude."

"Go 'dude' yourself. I paid you all I'm required to. Check the rules."

"I *did* check the rules. You owe me more!"

"I owe you nothing, buddy."

"Uh, yeah, you do. $1500. Pay up!"

Watching Jonty and Danny argue back and forth over the cluttered table of Monopoly pieces and fake money is sort of adorable, I have to admit. Over this past year, they've become like brothers—but the rowdy kind who can't stop bickering and fighting over every little thing. Then the next minute, the pair of them will make up and start laughing at something nonsensical. I don't understand it.

Prisha leans into me and whispers, "Should I cut in and play mediator again? Or …?"

"Nah, let them work it out."

"Are you sure?"

I shrug and give her a look. "Isn't it cute, though? Our boyfriends arguing with each other like an old married couple?"

"I always hated that saying," says Prisha thoughtfully. "Every 'old married couple' *I've* ever met get along like beautiful soul mates. We should stop the trend of thinking it's normal for couples to fight. We just need to learn how to communicate and accept our differences better."

I roll my eyes. "Do you *have* to turn everything into a poetic, philosophical curiosity?"

"Yes," answers Prisha rather matter-of-factly, still lost in her cloud of thoughts.

Across the table sits the fifth participant of tonight's game night: Elliot. Handsome yet weary-faced, with that glint of cocky authoritativeness in his eyes, and a cocktail hovering near his lips, his eyes play Ping-Pong between the arguing pair of Danny and Jonty. When he notices me looking at him, he smirks over his glass. "Is it weird if I'm sort of *shipping* your respective boyfriends to fuck someday?"

That very effectively silences both Danny and Jonty, who look his way, stunned.

"Meanwhile," Elliot goes on casually, "I have so much damned money, I'm willing to pay on Danny's behalf, just so we can carry the fuck on."

Jonty isn't having it. "That's not how the rules—"

"Does this beautiful face look like it cares?" asks Elliot, gesturing at said face with his cocktail glass. He grabs the money from his ghastly stash, slaps it in front of a bewildered Jonty, then nods at the board. "Besides, it's my turn next, and I've been eyeing a lovely hotel on Boardwalk for far too long. *A'hem.*" When there's no response, he clears his throat yet again. "I said: *A'hem.*"

The whole table jumps from a head suddenly bumping its underside. Then another face emerges from underneath—our sixth participant this evening: Tim. "Sir?"

"I need you to roll my dice," states Elliot rather lazily. "I'm still drinking and can't be bothered."

"Do you wish me to keep rubbing your feet, sir? Or—"

Elliot rolls his eyes. "No. I need my teammate up here to kick these guys' asses with a good roll of the dice!"

"Yes, sir!" Tim slips right into his chair as if he was sitting there the whole time, picks up the dice, and takes to rolling. The roll is less than adequate, landing them on a go-to-jail square. "S-Sorry, sir. I ... I seem to have made you unhappy."

"You should probably get back to my feet then until I'm back to being happy," Elliot decides. Tim vanishes the next moment while Elliot kicks back with a sigh, then shakes his head at us. "I swear, I don't ask for much. I'm reasonable. I keep my expectations low. Am I too demanding?"

The rest of us laugh, including Jonty and Danny, who seem to have settled on a truce of sorts. Soon, the rhythm of our game is restored, and we're back to playing without any further world-ending issues.

It's like this every Saturday night: a triple-date game night. Sometimes Elliot and Tim are absent, too busy doing their own thing—likely something kinky in the privacy of the apartment they got together a few months ago. But the remaining four of us look forward to it every weekend. Sometimes when it's just us four, we'll mix up the couples, with me and Prisha being on a team, and Danny and Jonty being on another. But quite often we're accused of cheating, since Prisha and I have a weird way of reading one another's minds during charades. We can't help it.

But after Monopoly, the six of us settle on the couch with some fresh drinks and a giant bowl of popcorn, and put on a classic movie everyone's seen ten times. Prisha and Jonty are cuddled up together on one side of the couch, now and then reciting a line they know, then snickering. Elliot is in the arm chair with Tim sitting on the floor in front of him, squeezed between Elliot's legs, still obsessed with pleasing him even during the movie.

Danny lies next to me at the other end of the couch with his head in my lap, where I gently stroke his hair, only half paying attention to the movie. Even after a whole year of being together, I catch myself wondering just how I possibly could deserve such happiness. Sometimes it feels like I'm living someone else's life, watching my contentment through a magic funhouse mirror.

Is this really my life?

"Of course it is," says Danny when we step out onto the fire escape together for a quick breath of fresh air. It's a slow part of the movie anyway. "Why would you doubt it?"

"I don't know. Maybe without the big, tough coldness of 'Romeo' guarding my heart anymore, I've been feeling rather vulnerable lately. Like I might … wake up someday, and … and realize I never deserved any of this." I turn to him. "Do you remember a year ago, when we went on that date, kinda our first 'real' date …"

"… and I lured you to my apartment for the first time where we finally made love?"

I smile. "Yes. That night. I was so afraid that was going to be a fluke … like our first *and* last night together."

"Really?"

"I thought maybe you'd realize I wasn't such a catch. Maybe I was as shallow as all of the meatheads and assholes and jerks that rotated through the gym like revolving doors. Maybe underneath the initial fascination, you'd realize … I wasn't much of a catch in the end."

"No, no, no." Danny takes my hand and pulls me closer to him. "Listen to me. If this past year with you has taught me anything, it's that you are *so* much more than a great catch. You're … how do I put this?" He smiles when it comes to him. "You're the most infuriating person I've ever known."

I pull back. "Say what?"

"You heard me." He smirks as he observes my reaction. "You're touchy sometimes. You get in a bad mood when your team disappoints you at work. You don't always clean up your hair in the shower."

"Eww, *yes*, I do."

"You hate doing dishes. You get, like … *irrationally* mad when you spot mistakes in news articles. You can't cook."

"Hey, now, I *can* make a mean bowl of Easy Mac ..."

"And you have weird taste in workout music." He brings his face close to mine. "And it's for literally all of those reasons that I love you, Romeo. Your imperfections. Your humanness. Your sweetness. Your overconfidence when you should be humble. And your modesty when you have a total right to brag. I love all of you, every part of you." He kisses me. "Romeo, you're more than just a good catch. You're *the* catch. You're the guy I've waited my whole life to find."

I bite my lip. "I'm still working out the shower thing, to be honest."

"And I'm irrevocably in love with you, Romeo."

"Like, I'm pretty sure I clean up after myself every night, and I—"

Danny shuts me right up with a kiss. I'm helpless to resist. You know you've found the right guy when he can win any argument with just a touch of his lips to yours.

And if I had any ability to respond right now, I'd return those words right back to him. Danny Chen, you're the man who saved me when no one else could. You're the guy I've waited my whole life to find. You're the antidote to every mean boy out there, whose hard shell is too tough for regular guys to crack.

The truth is, all they need is an angel like you, whose soul is so deep, whose heart is so boundless and free, whose spirit is so unwavering, even a tried-and-true jerk has no chance to resist you.

The end.

Other works by Daryl Banner

Spruce Texas Romances (M/M)
Football Sundae / Born Again Sinner / Heteroflexible / Wrangled
Rebel At Spruce High / Summer Sweat
(More coming soon…)

Boys & Toys (M/M)
Season 1: Caysen's Catch / Wade's Workout / Dean's Dare / Garret's Game
Season 2: Connor / Brett / Dante / Zak

The Brazen Boys (M/M)
Dorm Game / On The Edge / Owned By The Freshman
Dog Tags / All Yours Tonight / Straight Up
Houseboy Rules / Slippery When Wet / Commando: Dog Tags 2

Stand-alone Novels & Romances (M/M)
Bromosexual / Hard For My Boss / Getting Lucky / Raising Hell
My Bad Ex-Boyfriend / Lover's Flood: A Novel / When I See You Again
Making The Naughty List: A Magical Holiday Male/Male Romance
My Ghost Roommate (Who Helps Me Get The Guy)

A College Obsession Romance (M/F)
Read My Lips / Beneath The Skin / With These Hands
Through Their Eyes: Five Years Later

The Beautiful Dead Saga (Young Adult Fantasy)
The Beautiful Dead / Dead Of Winter / Almost Alive
The Whispers / Winter's Doom / Deathless

The OUTLIER Series (Dystopian)
Rebellion / Legacy / Reign Of Madness
Beyond Oblivion / Weapons Of Atlas / Gifts Of The Goddess

Kings & Queens: An OUTLIER Companion Series (Dystopian)
The Slum Queen / The Twice King / Queen Of Wrath

Made in USA - Kendallville, IN
45883_9798830558082
07.15.2022 1307